THE TUCKERS

Here Comes a Friend!

Exciting books about

THE TUCKERS

the Tuckers

Here Comes a Friend!

By
Jo Mendel

Pictures by
Jackie Tomes

WHITMAN PUBLISHING COMPANY
RACINE, WISCONSIN

CONTENTS

1
A Tucker Is Chosen

"Mother, Mother, *Mother!*" shrieked Merry Tucker.

Down Valley View Merry raced. Her heavy dark braids bounced on her shoulders. Nylon petticoats swirled. Her violin case banged her bare legs. Her music portfolio became totally unmanageable. Just as she reached the front gate of her home, Merry spilled her lesson book and several sheets of music on the sidewalk.

"Don't stop, Merry, I'll pick them up!" yelled Terry, her twin brother. He, too, bellowed, *"Mother!"* in a voice that popped open all the neighbors' doors.

From the Corbett and Jackson houses, even

11

from Pitchers' Grocery on the corner, people hurried out to call to each other, "What can be the matter? Is there a fire? An accident?"

Teen-aged Jim Jackson was mowing the lawn across the hedge from the Tucker house. His mother worked in a flower bed in her front yard. "Oh, dear, oh, dear, I do hope it's nothing serious," fretted Mrs. Jackson. She added her voice to the confusion and twittered, "Lois, Lois Tucker!"

Jim took one look at the twin-tangle at the Tucker gate. He chuckled, "It's Merry. It can be anything." Obligingly Jim cupped his hands around his mouth to make a megaphone. He roared, *"Mrs. Tucker!"*

"I'm in the backyard," answered Mother's voice.

"Thanks, Jim," Terry called.

Up the front walk and around the wide front porch raced the nine-year-old Tucker twins. Terry sashayed around a forsythia bush near the porch swing. He galloped at Merry's heels, picking up the music she dropped for the umpteenth time since she had left the Mitchell Grade School. Merry hobbled and wobbled past the living-room windows and around the corner of the big old house.

Completely out of breath, Merry came to an abrupt stop to keep from toppling Mother, who stood on a stepladder near the stone fireplace chimney.

Mother's anxious face peered through the great mass of purple lilacs she was cutting. "What's wrong, dear?" she asked. "Is there a tornado coming?"

Tom was balancing the stepladder for Mother. Carefully he examined his panting sister. In his deep, sober, older-than-five voice he observed, "I don't see anything coming." Then he added, "What's a tornado?"

"Oh, Tom," Mother laughed with a smile. She backed down the ladder, carefully shielding her armload of fragrant lilacs.

"M-Mother," Merry panted. "I—got—chosen." When she said the magic words her eyes became blue wells of happiness. Her red mouth made a round O of wonder.

"Yeah," Terry echoed. "Merry's name was called."

Mother's lips curved in an answering smile. "Tell me," she invited.

Merry hugged her violin case against her chest. She leaned one warm cheek against the battered leather. "My name was called," she told Mother, "to play in the all-school orchestra on recital night." Merry ended with a breathless rush of words.

"How about that?" Terry asked proudly.

"Indeed, how about that?" Mother repeated in a glow of love and pride. "Here, Tom, be a honey and put my lilacs in water, please?"

Obligingly Tom accepted the huge mass of purple flowers. He trotted to the back door beyond the fireplace chimney.

Mother put an arm across Merry's shoulders to urge her back around the house and up the wide porch steps to the big swing. Mother patted a pillow for Merry's back. But Merry sat on the edge of the swing, still hugging her violin case. The minute Mother and Terry sat down, Merry pushed her feet against the floor, setting the swing in motion.

Tom popped through the front door, unwilling

to miss a minute of Tucker fun and excitement.

Sugar, the cat, walked between Tom's feet. With dignity, Sugar crossed the porch. He wove in and out among the legs dangling from the swing. He purred loudly.

Toby, the ragamuffin Tucker dog, left his burrowed-out nest under the forsythia bush. He jumped onto the wide porch. When he lolled his tongue in a dog-laugh, bright eyes peered out of a mass of black and white curls.

Up the walk hurried the blond Tucker girls, Tina and Penny. Seven-year-old Penny tried to keep up with Tina's long legs.

"Merry, I just heard!" Tina called gladly. "I was in the library returning my book, and—"

"I was jumping rope," Penny put in, "and I came right away!"

With sober excitement Tom said, "Now, we're all here. Tell us, Merry."

With a jiggle of her shoulders, Merry explained, "I was coloring a map in my history

workbook, 'cause we have to turn it in tomorrow, and the door of our room opened, *and*—"
She paused dramatically.

"And what?" Penny urged.

"The *principal* walked in." Merry widened her blue eyes. Long black lashes pointed up at the unruly swoop of her dark brows. "And he called my *name*!"

"O-Oh," Penny said with a shiver. "Weren't you scared?"

Even Sugar seemed to wait for an answer. Sugar sat at Merry's feet. He stared at the wiggling curl at the end of one dark brown braid. Toby saw a chance to join the group. He scrambled into the space in the porch swing behind Merry and breathed down her neck.

Merry moved layers of nylon petticoats and her plaid gingham skirt as she made room for Toby's big feet. Then she went on as if there had been no interruption. "I wasn't scared— just surprised."

Terry bobbed his head. He sat across the aisle from Merry in the fourth grade. Hearing Merry's name called by the principal was almost like hearing his own. Well, almost—but not quite.

"And he said," Merry hurried on, " 'Merry Tucker has been selected to represent Mitchell School in the violin section on recital night.' And he walked down the aisle, and he shook my hand, and he gave me a number—"

Merry put down her violin with a clatter. Frantically she pawed through her music in the portfolio on Terry's lap. "Did I lose it?" she wailed. "Did I lose my *number*? I have to wear it, every time we practice, and on recital night, *too*!"

"I see it," Tom said calmly. His hand reached in among Terry's and Merry's fingers. He picked up a white cardboard with a hole punched near the top edge. "What's the hole for?" Tom wanted to know.

"That's for a ribbon," Merry explained, "to go around my neck."

Tom's lips pursed. He pulled his brows into his thinking look. "You'll punch it with your bow and get all tangled up I bet," he said at last.

"Oh, Mother, I might!" Merry wailed.

The whole family looked at Tom with respect. He did not go to school, but he had the kind of mind which went straight to the root of a problem. Anybody could see that a violin bow tangled in a ribbon around Merry's neck while hundreds and hundreds of people watched would be a problem.

"We'll fix it," Mother promised comfortingly. She reached for the card. "Five hundred and fifty-one?" she read. Her voice lifted in a question. "My word, how many children are in the recital?"

"Oh, lots," Tina told Mother. "There will be an orchestra, and a band, and a chorus."

"From all the schools from Yorkville to Castleton," Terry put in.

Tom looked down the street. His eyes seemed to count the number of schools. "High schools, too?" he asked. "Is Jim Jackson going to be in it?"

Merry giggled at the idea of their long-legged basketball hero in her orchestra. "Just grade school music pupils."

"Well, that's enough," Mother declared. "Five hundred. My word!"

Merry whirled to face Mother. "Oh, there are more than five hundred!"

Tina tapped her fingers while she added numbers for Mother. "Two hundred in the chorus," she said. "And three hundred in the band. And one hundred and forty in the orchestra."

"Don't forget all the folk dancers," Terry reminded them.

"And there'll be one hundred folk dancers," Tina added.

"And ushers," Merry prompted.

"And all the music teachers," Terry said.

Mother put her hands over her ears. "Stop, stop!" she begged. "I'll have to see it to believe it."

"Betcha we'll hear 'em," Tom said wisely.

Terry winked at his pre-school brother. "Betcha," he agreed.

At that moment Sugar decided he had been left out long enough. He jumped into Mother's lap. Mother's lashes did not even flutter. She was used to life on a merry-go-round of sound and action. She smoothed one of Sugar's ears, split in some long ago cat fight. When Sugar curled into a comfortable ball, Mother asked Merry, "How many violins will play in the orchestra?"

Blissfully Merry clasped her thin, long-fingered hands and stared at the porch ceiling. "One hundred and twenty," she answered. "Isn't it wonderful? I'm *one* of them."

"Yeah, you and one hundred nineteen others," Terry said. He jumped up unexpectedly. Sheets of music scattered all over the floor. Toby almost fell out of the swing. "Who's for a game of catch in the play-field?" Terry asked.

Tom was sitting on the floor with his back against the wall under a wide front window. Instantly he unfolded his sturdy legs. "I'm ready," he declared.

Both boys clattered down the steps. Terry

turned to look up at his twin. "Wanta play?" he invited.

"Oh—" Merry started to refuse, but something in Terry's face made her agree. "Just as soon as I put on my jeans." With a swoop of both hands she collected the sheets of music. She shoved them back into her portfolio and picked up her violin case.

"Don't hurt your fingers, Merry," Mother cautioned. When Merry slammed the front screen door, Mother turned to Terry. "Don't throw the ball too hard," she warned.

Terry swaggered. "I'll be careful. She's just a girl."

Tom defended Merry. "Merry can catch any ball you can throw, Terry Tucker."

Quick color ran up Terry's cheeks. He started to scowl. Tom's eyes were so unflinching, Terry laughed instead. "Why shouldn't Merry be good? She's my twin!"

With a whoop which raised Mrs. Jackson from

her work in her flower bed, Terry ran down the
walk and through the front gate. "Play ball!" he
shouted as he headed for the play-field at the
end of the dead-end street.

2

An Invisible Door

Before Father came home from work the neighbors "just happened" to drop in. Even Mrs. Pitcher came. She seldom left the little neighborhood grocery store on the corner. She bustled down the block to see why the twins had run all the way home from school. Tina called Merry home from the play-field to tell her own story.

Merry sat on the big leather hassock near the fireplace. With every other sentence she drummed her heels to let out another burst of excitement. Tom and Penny crowded onto the hassock with Merry—Tina turned about on the piano bench to face Merry. Mother presided at the tea cart on wheels. She made only the tiniest

tinkle with china and silver. But Terry leaned
one shoulder against the face of the fireplace and
thumped a softball into his catcher's mitt.

"Isn't it exciting to have Merry chosen to play
in the recital?" Mrs. Jackson asked.

Silence dropped into the middle of the chir-
ruping conversation. Terry bunched his dark
brows and played ball with himself. Thump.
Thump. Thump. Then he became aware that
eyes were looking at him. Mother's blue eyes
were cool with disapproval.

"Huh?" Terry gasped. Suddenly he realized
it was he, and not Merry, who was being ques-
tioned. " 'Scuse me?"

Patiently Mother repeated Mrs. Jackson's
question.

"Oh. Oh, sure," Terry gulped. "It's nice, Mrs.
Jackson."

"Will you play in the band, Terry?" Mrs. Corbett asked.

Terry watched the second-door-neighbor stir

a sugar cube in her tea. Before Terry found words, Tom told Mrs. Corbett, "Terry didn't practice."

Heat ran up Terry's cheeks. "Tat—" he burst out, then tightened his jaws. He was not being fair. Tom was not a tattletale. Tom had simply stated a fact. Terry had not taken the time to memorize the music handed out many months ago.

Terry's sense of humor came to his rescue. "There are four hundred and forty better musicians," he admitted with a twisted little grin. "And Merry is one of them."

"Oh, Terry, I'm not better than you are," Merry protested loyally. "I just—"

"—practiced," Terry finished his twin's sentence. In the mirror behind the davenport he saw Mrs. Pitcher nod at Mrs. Jackson, who turned to smile at Mrs. Corbett. It restored Terry's self-confidence for the moment. He put down his mitt and softball and walked to the tea cart. "May I pass the cookies, Mother?" he asked.

Terry was rewarded with a bright smile. "Would you, please, Terry?" Mother asked.

While he circled the room with a plate of Tina's pecan bars, Terry kept glancing back at Merry. He had been the one to close his workshop door and hang out a sign, "No Girls Allowed." He had objected to Merry's tagging the play-field gang. He had locked up his bicycle. When Merry even looked at his miniature cars, he yelled.

There were more girls than boys in the Tucker family, and one of them was his twin. Terry had given himself the right to push out Merry whenever it pleased him, just to make a balance between boys and girls. Now a door had been shut in his own face. Not an attic door, but an invisible door with no knob.

Terry's heart told him there should be no door between twins.

Ever since the principal's announcement, Terry had felt himself shrinking, while Merry grew and grew like something out of Wonderland. At first he had not minded. Now Terry's heart became so heavy his feet dragged. Terry was glad when Father pushed open the screen door and entered the front hall. Terry had wondered how he could possibly cross that wide, wide space between Mrs. Corbett's chair and Mother's tea cart. Quickly Terry turned to Father. The remaining pecan bars slid about on the plate. "Have a cooky, Father?" Terry invited.

"Mmm, good," Father mumbled hungrily. "Did Tina bake these?" He smiled with pride when Terry nodded.

Father hung his hat and jacket in the clothes closet under the open stairs. He smoothed his dark hair with one hand. Then he turned towards the living room. Father paused when he faced Mrs. Pitcher on the window seat instead of

behind a grocer's counter. "Company?" Father observed with a smile. "Nice to see you, Mrs. Pitcher."

"Everybody is here, Father," Penny called. She ran across the rug. When her white flats touched bare hardwood, Penny slid into Father's arms. Father gave Penny an affectionate hug. Holding his youngest daughter's hand, he advanced to meet his family and neighbors.

After a friendly twitter of feminine voices, the neighbors prepared to leave. Each assured Merry, "Remind us of the date, dear. We'll certainly attend."

"Attend?" Father repeated when Mother went to the door with the guests. "Attend what, Merry?"

"Oh, Father," Merry burst out. "You'll never guess!"

Father grinned down at Merry's excited face. "Then tell me," he suggested.

Again Merry told her story, complete with

arm waving. Almost against his will, Terry watched and listened.

Secretly Terry did not agree with Merry's report card. He considered his twin the smartest girl in the fourth grade, and the prettiest, though he would not tell her so. She wore her curly, dark brown hair in heavy, bouncing braids. Slim and quick-moving, red-cheeked and blue-eyed, Merry glowed with good health and good humor. When she smiled, a fellow just had to smile back at her, as Father was smiling now.

Terry sighed. He reached for his mitt and soft-ball. Carefully he kept his eyes on the little leather well in the middle of the mitt. Thump, went his ball. Thump. Thump.

Merry talked on and on.

Mother returned to the tea cart. She sent Tina to the kitchen for the glass of milk Father liked when he came home from work. Mother nodded and smiled and looked proud. Several times Father's hand reached for a cooky. While he listened to Merry, he traded pleased smiles with Mother. Obviously Bill and Lois Tucker were proud to be Merry's parents.

Briefly Terry wondered how they would have acted if his name had been called. Then Terry shut his mind.

When Merry ran out of words, Father asked, "Won't you have to spend a lot of time practicing?"

"Oh, no, Father," Merry answered earnestly. "The recital is next week."

"With over seven hundred children in the program?" Father whistled and shook his head.

"We *know* our parts," Merry assured Father. "We'll just have to put them together."

"That I'll have to hear," Father said. His mouth twitched at a corner when he looked from Merry to Mother.

Mother left the room and soon sounds came from the kitchen. Tina hurried to pick up the teacups. She pushed the tea cart into the kitchen and began to help Mother prepare the dinner.

Terry took the last cooky from the plate when Tina passed his chair and then moved to the window seat. There he broke the cooky in several parts and fed them to Toby in exchange for tricks. The big dog scrambled when he rolled over the third time for only a sniff at Terry's fingers.

"That's not fair, Terry," Merry protested. "When Toby does a trick, you should feed him."

"Not till he does it right," Terry insisted.

Father's eyes traveled over Terry's face. "Something bothering you, son?" he asked.

"No, sir," Terry muttered. He clapped his hands to tell Toby the treat was gone. Then Terry escaped to the front porch. There he waited for the paper boy who was ambling down Valley View, rolling papers and shouting to his customers.

With the evening paper in his hands, Terry

wandered through the hall, past the foot of the front stairs and into the kitchen. Mother and Tina were preparing dinner. He spread sheets on the breakfast table and concentrated on the comics. Tom joined Terry and studied the strips, frame by frame, while Terry read the conversation aloud.

Tom's deep voice rumbled out of the bottom of his throat, "You don't sound funny tonight, Terry."

Terry shrugged and left the paper spread all over the table top. Silently he opened a can of cat food for Sugar. After that he went to the backyard and he bounced his ball at the side of the garage.

Tom could not read, but he managed to get a lot of information from a newspaper by studying the pictures. "Here's a boy with a violin," Tom told Mother and Tina. "He's about as big as Tina."

"Then he must be the same age," Mother

answered.

"Maybe he's in the recital," Tina suggested eagerly. "Let me see, Tom." Tina left the green salad she was chopping. With one arm around Tom's waist, Tina leaned over the newspaper.

She read aloud, " 'Colin Whitney Blake, aged eleven, son of Senator and Mrs. Whitney Blake of Castleton, will appear in recital in the York-ville Coliseum on May 29.' " Outrage shone in Tina's blue eyes. "Mother!" she gasped. "That sounds like that boy is going to play the whole recital by himself. That isn't fair."

Mother wrapped her wet hands in a towel. She joined Tom and Tina. She, too, looked at the picture and read the news item. Then she suggested, "Maybe there are pictures of other children in a different section of the paper."

Tina fluttered through all the sheets. "No," she said.

"Yes, there is," Tom said. He jabbed a finger at a picture Tina had missed.

Tina flattened the paper. She bent her head beside Mother's to read the story under the picture of a number of children on the steps of the Chesterfield Blake grade school. The same boy, wearing smartly tailored slacks and jacket, stood in the middle of the group. The creases of his slacks hung straight. The toes of his shoes glistened and his dark hair was neatly parted and smoothly brushed.

"Blake," Mother said thoughtfully. "He must

be a member of the family that school was named for. That would be my guess."

"Does he have to have his picture in the paper twice when there are dozens of other kids in the recital?" Tina asked hotly.

"Hundreds, you mean," Mother corrected. She returned to the sink and picked up her paring knife. While she peeled a potato she suggested mildly, "Maybe he's good."

"Not that good," Tina declared, "or we'd have heard of him."

Mother's shoulders moved in a small shrug. "The Blakes are in the news quite often. Whitney Blake is one of our senators, you know."

"Really?" Tina asked. She looked at the picture with new interest. She had received an A in American history and was much impressed with anybody who made laws others had to obey.

"What's a senator?" Tom asked.

"A man who helps to make our laws," Mother told him.

"Like a policeman," Tom said.

"Oh, no!" Tina objected. "A senator is *very* important. *He* gets elected, not hired."

Tom considered Tina's words. He did not know what she meant, but he could see she thought this Senator Blake was somebody Father and Grandfather would call "sir." That must make his son important, too. Thoughtfully Tom studied the picture of the children on the steps. After a silence he declared, "That boy's name sounds like a girl's name."

"Yes, I suppose it does," Mother agreed, "but lots of names belong to both girls and boys— Carol, Billy, Lee, Frances, Gale—"

Tina chanted while she chopped spinach on the salad board, "Dean, Claire, Jay."

Mother giggled and interrupted: "Jan, Shirley, Nicky, Gerry, Lynn, Raye, Laurie. Oh, dear, I've run out of names!"

Tina shouted, "Bobby, Jean, Faye, Tommy—"

"My name isn't a girl's name!" Tom insisted.

With both hands clenched into fists he marched across the room. He looked up into Mother's face. "Is my name a girl's name, Mother?" he demanded fiercely.

"No, Tom," Mother assured the worried, small boy. "Your name is Thomas. I've never heard of a girl named Thomas. Thomas Tucker is a man's name."

Tom stared levelly at Tina. "See?" he demanded.

Father came into the kitchen. He leaned on a doorjamb. He fished celery chunks from the salad and chewed while he listened. "What's the discussion?" he asked.

Mother washed the potatoes and plopped them into a saucepan, then stooped to peek through the glass oven door at the meat loaf. "Senator Blake's son, Colin, is playing violin in the recital at the coliseum," Mother told Father.

"And he's eleven, same as Tina," Tom added. His deep, sober voice, which would some day equal Grandpa's deep bass, seemed to add importance to his words.

"Do you suppose Merry will meet that Blake boy?" Tina asked.

Father shrugged and reached for a carrot stick. "She might," he agreed good-naturedly. "So what?"

"So what?" Tina echoed. "Colin Whitney Blake has his picture in the paper twice on the same night, that's what!"

"Does it make him somebody special?" Father teased with a twinkle in his eye.

"It must," Tina declared soberly. "Merry has never had her picture in the paper, and she's going to play in that program, too."

3
Assignment for Tom

Father entered the kitchen where the older children were eating breakfast. Mother looked up from the toaster. "I'll fry your eggs in just one minute, Bill. Merry has to be at school at eight."

"No hurry, honey," Father told her. Smelling of shaving lotion and shoe polish, he circled the table. He left a kiss on each girl's forehead. He clapped Terry's shoulder. Father paused to grin down at Tom, who was sprawled on the floor. A picture window overlooked the backyard. Its light fell on the morning newspaper.

"Anything in the news I should know about?" Father asked Tom.

"There was a train wreck, and I s'pose the President made a speech—there's his mike." Tom explained the pictures he was poring over. "And that boy with the girl's name did something else."

"Colin Whitney Blake?" Tina asked alertly.

Merry's fork clattered to her plate. "Tom, let me see," she demanded. "Maybe I'll see him at practice this morning."

Tom gathered up the paper and held it in front of Merry. Both Tina and Merry twisted in their chairs to look at the picture of the Blake boy. He was smiling at a pretty blond girl, who was giving a bouquet to a woman wearing a fur stole. Senator Blake stood behind the children, smiling proudly.

Quickly Tina read the words under the picture. She announced, "That girl is Colin Whitney Blake's cousin."

There was something perky and self-assured about the girl. A mass of curls lay high on her forehead and a heavy ponytail fell from the top of her head.

"She doesn't look real," Merry whispered in awe. "She looks like a doll on a Christmas tree."

"I wonder who combs her hair," Tina mused.

Curiosity overcame Terry's usual lack of interest in girl-stuff. He stood up to look over Merry's shoulder. "Huh, flowers." He snorted and sat down to finish his eggs.

Merry gulped the last drop of milk in her tumbler. Then she raced up the back stairs and down again, to the front hall closet and back, to the living-room window seat and back to the breakfast table. "Now!" she said breathlessly. "I'm ready."

"Got your number?" Tom asked calmly.

"Oh!" Merry squealed. "I forgot to put it on a ribbon!" Back up the stairs she raced. Almost instantly she shrieked, "Mother, I can't find a ribbon! A hair ribbon is too wide!"

Mother called, "Look in the second drawer

under the window in the sewing room."

Father chuckled. "Bull in a china shop, that's our Merry."

Tom slid into his chair and picked up his paper napkin. Loyally he told Father, "Anyway, Merry can play violin."

Father tousled Tom's short brown hair. "That she can, Tom."

Almost at once Tina and Merry returned to the kitchen. Merry wore number 551 on a narrow red ribbon. She gathered up her violin case, portfolio, and school books. She flashed a bright smile at the family. " 'Bye!" she said happily.

Mother rose to kiss Merry's cheek. She pushed a bobby pin into the top of one fat, dark braid. "Good luck, dear," she said.

Terry stared at his plate till Merry reached the back door. Then he pushed back his chair. "Merry, I'll carry your stuff," he offered gruffly. After the twins left, Tina looked thoughtful. She scraped breakfast plates and put them in

the sink. "Have you burned the newspapers late-
ly, Mother?" she asked.

"No, dear, they're in a box in the furnace
room."

Tina sighed with relief. She turned to Tom
and coaxed, "Will you do something for me today,
please, Tom?"

Tom liked to help. "Sure," he agreed.

"Will you look at the pictures in the old newspapers and cut out any you can find of the
Blakes?"

Tom looked pleased with the assignment.
"That'll take all morning," he said, "and maybe
all afternoon, too." His eyes shone with interest.

Father winked at Tom, then spoke across the
kitchen to Tina. "You put that job in good hands,
Tina. But why this sudden interest in the
Blakes?"

"Because I've never met a senator's son," Tina
answered. Her eyes widened as she tried to imag-
ine the daily life of a man so important his

actions were news. Why, to be a senator's son must be a little bit like being a prince!

Dreamily Tina added, "And his cousin is *so* pretty."

Tom excused himself and pushed his chair into place. He asked, "Are you going to use the laundry table, Mother?"

Mother smiled over her lifted coffee cup. "Help yourself, Tom," she agreed. "The basement is all yours today."

"Be sure to refold the papers," Father cautioned.

"Sure," Tom said.

Merry was last to reach home for lunch. She was barely inside the door when Tina darted out of the living room. "Did you see him?" Tina asked eagerly.

"Wh-who?" Merry stammered.

"The senator's son," Tina returned impatiently.

"I *think* so," Merry said doubtfully, "but there were so many kids and we had to do just what we were told, and find our seats, and watch the director *very* carefully, and—"

"Merry, how did your orchestra sound?" Mother called from the kitchen.

"Awful!" Merry answered with a remembering giggle. "But Mr. Jones says we'll make real music next week."

"That's all that matters," Mother agreed. "Lunch is ready, everybody."

Merry, Terry, and Tina quickly seated themselves around the kitchen table. Tom came up the basement stairs. Hands, face, and even bare legs were smudged with dust and printer's ink.

"What have you been doing, Tom?" Merry asked. "Playing in the coal bin?" Hungrily she bit into a tuna fish sandwich while she watched Tom wash his hands at the kitchen sink and wipe with a paper towel.

"I've been working," Tom said with dignity.

"And I can spell Blake. B-l-a-k-e."

Merry gulped. "Why did you learn to spell Blake?"

"So I could work," Tom said soberly. He tilted his head to look up at Tina. He asked, "What does S-e-n spell?"

"It means senator," Tina told him.

"Oh." Tom looked wise.

"Maybe you two know what you're talking about, but I don't," Merry declared. She picked up her soup spoon. She moved her soup plate closer to the edge of the table.

"Watch it, Merry," Terry warned. "You'll douse your braids in your soup."

Merry wrinkled her nose at her twin. "Then I'll be the only girl in school with tomato-colored braids." Cheerfully she flipped her braids over her shoulder. She reached for a second sandwich.

Mother passed a plate of orange slices and quartered apples. No time remained for Tina and Tom to explain their discussion.

While they hastily brushed teeth, Tina urged Merry, "Hurry home from school."

"Can't," Merry bubbled through her toothpaste. "Have to catch the bus to the coliseum."

"Oh." Tina felt a twinge of disappointment, quickly forgotten when she glanced in the mirror. "I wonder," she mused, "how I would look with a ponytail and bangs."

Tina thought about her hair all afternoon. The minute she got home she hurried upstairs to the girls' bathroom and locked the door. Carefully she combed about a third of her hair down over her face. She dampened the hair and proceeded to roll it into tight, lumpy pincurls. These were anchored with dozens of bobby pins. Next she set to work on the rest of her hair. Tina's hair was fine and silky. The more she brushed, the more it slid. It was not easy to hold her blond mane straight up from the top of her head long enough to put a rubber band around it. Finally she gave up. "Penny," she called, "come help me."

Usually Penny rested the first half hour after school. Tina listened and sighed with relief. Penny pattered across the floor of the room she shared with Merry.

"I can't get in," Penny said through the door.

"Oh, 'scuse me, I'll unlock it," Tina said. She held her neck stiff as a ruler while she opened the door.

When she saw Tina, Penny's mouth fell open. Wordlessly she let her eyes travel up Tina's arm to the hair she held straight up like a kewpie's topknot.

Hastily Tina explained, "I want you to tie a ribbon for me."

A wall rack held the rainbow collection of ribbons worn by the three girls. Penny chose a blue one.

While Tina watched in the mirror, Penny tied

the ribbon as close to Tina's head as she could manage. Penny winced with sympathy when she tied some long blond hairs in the knot.

Tina was too impatient for results to notice the hurt. "Do you like it?" she asked Penny.

Worriedly Penny walked around Tina. "The back hairs won't stay up," she answered.

"Put pins in," Tina urged. She bent her slim neck while Penny labored with bobby pins. Quickly Tina put on the hood of the small electric hair dryer. She settled herself in the blue bath-room chair. A small smile lifted the corners of her soft, pink mouth. She pictured herself as flawlessly groomed as Colin Whitney Blake's cousin. And, oh, she would be pretty!

Penny brought Tina's library book. She left the bathroom door open while she returned to her bed. Once in the while Tina or Penny spoke softly. Most of the time a friendly silence closed around them. The clock on Merry's bedside table clicked. Penny's lids grew heavier and heavier.

She was just on the rim, ready to fall into the deep well of sleep, when Tina said briskly, "Time's up." Penny jerked awake. She sat straight up in bed. For the moment she had forgotten about Tina's hair. Her eyes widened when Tina took off the hood of the hair dryer.

"How do I look?" Tina asked eagerly.

"L-Like a pincushion with a darning needle stuck in it," Penny giggled sleepily.

Tina hurried to the mirror and began to pull out bobby pins. She called through the door to Penny, "Just you wait until I comb out my bangs."

"You didn't cut your hair?" Penny asked in alarm. She raced across the bedroom and into the bathroom.

"Not yet," Tina said.

"Oh, I wouldn't," Penny warned. "Mother wouldn't like it."

While Penny watched, Tina began to comb out the pincurls. Oh, she was going to look

exactly like the senator's niece, and that was as pretty as a Christmas doll.

With each curl combed, a little light went out of Tina's eyes. Some curls fell down. Others developed sprouts which stuck into the air. Not one looked like the perfect layers of that cousin's bangs. Tina used the hand mirror to study her head from all sides. "I'm not pretty, am I, P-Penny?" she quavered.

"You are, but your ponytail isn't," Penny said

truthfully. Penny liked for everybody around her to be happy. So she added, "Maybe Mother can fix it for you."

"I don't want her to see it," Tina gulped unhappily.

Tenderhearted Penny's eyes filled with tears, too. "What'll you do, Tina?"

Tina's chin raised. Her usual good sense took control of her vanity. "I'll wash my hair and have Mother roll the ends the way she always does."

Penny smiled. "Then you'll be pretty."

Feet pounded up the back stairs. Tina's hands flew to the top of her head to cover up her odd hairdo. "Shut the door, quick," she begged Penny. "I can't let Terry see me. He'll call me a cockatoo!"

Penny giggled. "You do look like a skinny bird with a topknot," she agreed.

Not Terry, but Tom spoke through the bath-room door. He sounded pleased. "My work is done, Tina," he rumbled from the bottom of his throat.

"Good!" Tina told Tom, but she cast a wistful glance at the mirror. She wanted so much to be pretty.

4
B-l-a-k-e!

When the front door slammed, Penny was in the girls' bathroom watching Mother roll Tina's wet hair. Following the closing of the door, there was not another sound.

After a while Mother said, "That must be Merry, but I wonder what she's doing."

"I'll go see," Penny offered. She hurried through Tina's bedroom, into the hall, past the head of the back stairs, and down the front stairs to the landing. There Penny leaned on the railing. She looked down into the wide front hall.

Merry sat hunched in a chair by the door. She hugged her violin case. Her chin rested on the leather, and her eyes had a glazed look.

"Merry's just sitting," Penny called back to Mother.

Almost at once Mother and Tina joined Penny on the landing. Tina clutched a blue towel around her wet hair. They looked down at Merry. "What's wrong, Merry?" Mother asked anxiously.

Merry raised her eyes but did not move. "I'm tired," she muttered.

Mother hurried down the steps. One hand slid on the banister. She *tsk-tsked* with her tongue. "Are you sure all this practice isn't too much for you, Merry, right at the end of school?"

Just the suggestion that anything was too much for a Tucker seemed to revive Merry. She leaned her violin case against a wall. She jumped up.

"It was fun, Mother, really," Merry insisted brightly. "But my arm is about to fall off from all that bowing. Mr. Jones says my pizzicato is just fine. I get to sit in the front row! But there is another girl who is better with vibrato, so she gets to sit next to the audience."

Merry stopped chattering. She fluttered her fingers at the kitchen door beyond the foot of the front stairs. "Hi, Tom," she said cheerfully.

"Wanta see my work?" he invited.

"When Mother finishes my hair," Tina promised. "Is that all right?"

"Sure," Tom agreed. "Call me when you're ready."

Tom shared a cooky with Toby in exchange for tricks while he waited. When Tina called, he brightened. He had worked hard and was proud of what he had done. "Come on," he invited. Mother and the three girls followed him down the basement stairs. When he reached the laundry table. Tom waited for comments.

A few clippings and a pair of blunt scissors lay in a straight line on the table.

"Oh, my!" Tina gasped. "Tom, I didn't know

you would find so many pictures."

"And he folded the papers," Penny said proudly.

"Tom, you *did* learn to read Blake." Merry spoke with such excited surprise, Tom flushed with pleasure.

He trotted to the end of the table and picked up two clippings. "I am sure about these," Tom told Tina. "I can see the faces." He pursed his lips. His dark brows drew together when he waved at the rest of the clippings. "But I didn't know about those. They say Blake, but some of them don't look right. One man is wearing a clown suit." Tom turned to Mother. "Do senators wear clown suits?"

Mother smiled at Tom's serious question. "May I see the picture, Tom?"

Gravely Mother took the picture Tom gave her. Her eyes danced, but her voice was as sober as Tom's face. She scanned the news item. Mother told Tom, "You're right, Tom. This Mr.

Blake is a leader in a Boy Scout circus."

Merry and Tina had been edging along the laundry table. Merry giggled. "Here's a man named Blake who held up a gas station."

"And this Blake family has to move because the new freeway takes their land," Tina read with interest.

"What did this boy do?" Penny asked Merry.

"He won a freckle contest!" Merry giggled so hard she leaned against Tina.

Tom interrupted his sisters. With dignity he told them, "I told you I wasn't sure about those. These are right." He held out two newspaper clippings.

Tina took the pictures. One showed the senator, broad-chested and tall, in front of a microphone. Behind him stood a well-dressed woman and a boy with alert dark eyes.

In the second picture the boy sat astride a sleek horse. Colin Whitney Blake was obviously tall for his age—a dark, lean boy who looked quite a bit older than eleven.

"Oh, my—" Both Tina and Merry let their voices fade in admiration.

Mother and Penny looked at the pictures, too. Mother walked along the table and picked up the picture of a building. "Here's the senator's house," Mother said. With interest she added, "It's on Lake Annabelle."

Tom, Tina, Penny, and Merry crowded close. Grandpa Tucker had a cottage on Lake Annabelle. The Tuckers loved every inch of the lake, the shore, and the woods which sloped back to farm land. "Let's see!" they cried.

Merry was first to recognize the property. "I know where that house is," she bubbled. "You go past the store, and across the bay to the country club, and—"

"I know!" Tina interrupted. "It's the house that looks like a castle set right down on the edge of the water. It has twin towers and a big lawn on the hill behind the house."

Tom poked out his lower lip. Disgustedly he said, "I remember, too. Their basement is in the lake. Anybody knows that's a silly way to build a house."

Mother chuckled. "That house is supposed to be a copy of a house in Venice where they have canals for streets."

Tom failed to understand. "I'll bet those Blakes have water in their basement," he declared. "Grandfather's cottage is nicer. It's dry."

Mother hugged Tom. "You funny, sensible boy," she said with a catch in her voice. "I think you're right. Grandfather's cottage is nicer."

Merry gasped, "Nicer than the Blakes' house?"

"Oh, Mother!" Tina cried. "Their house is a *mansion!*"

Tom's deep voice asked, "What's a mansion?"

After the briefest of pauses, Mother shrugged prettily. She echoed, "Yes, girls, can you answer

Tom? What's a mansion?"

"A big house—" Tina began breathlessly. Then she repeated, "A big, big house." In her mind she built a house big enough and fine enough to shelter the girl with the perfect pony-tail, and the boy with the alert eyes, the tall woman, and the senator. Since she imagined a senator's son to be like a young prince, she was glad that the big house on Lake Annabelle had towers.

"The next time we go to the lake, I'm going to see that house," Tina finished.

The days melted like chocolate in the sun. Suddenly it was May 29, the last day of school and the date of the all-school recital which had taken so much of Merry's time.

Dressed in their best summer clothes, the Tuckers walked up Valley View to receive their report cards and say good-bye to their school friends.

Tom went with them. He visited the sixth

grade to watch Tina receive a prize. She had
read the most library books during the school
year, and her prize was a book. It did not interest
Tom after he discovered there were no pictures.
Tina's blue eyes glowed. Every few seconds, she
peeked. "I'll read it aloud," she promised Tom.

After Tina received her card, all A's excepting
in arithmetic, she took Tom to the fourth grade
room. There he shared a seat with Terry. While
Terry and Merry walked up the aisle for their

cards, Tom folded his hands. He pretended this was his desk. But when Terry returned and whispered his grade list, Tom was glad this was not his desk. Some day, when he sat at this desk, Tom Tucker would earn better grades!

The teacher wished Merry the best of luck in the recital. She told her, "We're proud of you Merry. I hope you do even better next year!" She sparkled at the room, at the teacher, and at all of her classmates. Then Merry took Tom down the hall to visit Penny.

When Tom joined Penny, she whispered, "I thought you would never come. Everybody else has already stood up."

While Penny was still whispering, her teacher said, "I see Penny's brother has arrived. Penny, dear, would you like to introduce him to the class?"

Tom was not quite sure what was expected of him. He sat very straight, ready for anything.

Penny bustled into the aisle. She wore so many

stiff petticoats her skirt curved like a blue bell. She twisted her thin hands into a knot. She fidgeted her feet. Then Penny took a deep breath. She burst out, all in one sentence, "This is Tom, he's my brother, and he is smarter'n me, and he wants to go to school but he can't 'cause he isn't old enough!" Penny gasped, ready to rush on.

But the teacher said, with a smile, "That's a fine introduction, Penny. We wish Tom were old enough to go to school, don't we, class?"

Several children said, "Yes!"

Tom felt a warm rush of affection for Penny. "I'm not smarter'n you," he rumbled deep in his throat.

"Ssh," Penny warned. "We can't talk out loud. But you *are* smarter, Tom. *I* can't spell Blake."

Tom moved his lips. He mumbled, "B-l-a-k-e," to be sure he had not forgotten.

Although he had never seen a member of the Blake family, they seemed to belong to Tom. He was the one who had found the picture of Colin

Whitney Blake and his violin. The whole family, even Father, had been interested to learn the Blakes lived on Lake Annabelle. "Maybe I'll see one of those Blakes sometime," Tom mused.

Tom would recognize them. He had memorized the shapes of their faces, the way they stood, and the kind of clothes they wore.

When the boys and girls of the second grade stood up, Tom stood up, too. They sang a song about "Little Tom Tinker." When they said Tom, they grinned at Tom Tucker. This made Tom wish he knew the song, too. After that, they sang, "Be you to others kind and true, and always unto others do as you'd have others do to you." Then they held the hands of their smaller brothers and sisters and bustled down the aisles.

Tom did not like to have his hand held, but he knew Penny would be embarassed if he said anything. So Tom let Penny hold his hand so tight it felt sticky. He edged down the aisle. He tried to

make room for Penny's blue skirt and all the stiff
petticoats.

"I'll look forward to having you in my class,
Tom Tucker," Penny's pretty teacher told him.
He felt so pleased with the last-day excitement
at school, he let Penny hold his hand all the way
to the water fountain in the hall.

Then Tom mumbled, "Gotta get a drink." He
pulled free from Penny's clutching fingers. Tom
wiped his mouth and stepped back into the line

again. He stuck his hands in his pockets. That was to let Penny know he weighed more than she did, even though she was taller and went to school.

Besides, he could spell B-l-a-k-e.

5
The Unexpected Musician

Since Merry had to be in her chair by seven o'clock, Father went with her on the Lincoln Avenue bus. That left the station wagon for Mother's use.

When Mother backed the rattley old blue station wagon down the drive, Toby galloped close to the left rear wheel. Toby lolled his long red tongue.

"Stay home!" Terry said sternly. Toby sat down and hung his head.

"Oh, Terry," tenderhearted Penny wailed, "you've hurt Toby's feelings."

Toby recognized a sympathetic voice. He straightened and flopped his curly bangs. He peered at the car door which stood ajar while Tina checked locked doors for Mother. Tina joined Tom and Penny in the middle seat. When she shut the door in his face, Toby drooped, and looked very sad.

"We'll be back soon. Be a good dog," Penny called through an open window.

Slowly Mother backed into the street. Watchfully, Toby followed. The minute the car began to roll, Toby galloped down the middle of the street.

"Stop, Mother!" chorused the Tuckers.

Mother pulled to the curb in front of Jim Jackson's house. Terry opened his door. With a happy toss of curls, Toby scurried around the station wagon. When he tried to climb in, Terry said firmly, "Stay, Toby! Stay."

Again Mother started the car. This time Toby hunched by the Jacksons' hedge.

"Toby's crying," Tom rumbled.

"He'll just have to cry," Mother declared. "We

must not be late to Merry's program. With so
many children in tonight's recital, the downtown
traffic is going to be heavy."

With careful attention to ruffles and creases,
the Tuckers settled back for the drive to the
coliseum. Several times Tom rolled down his window and craned his neck. Once Tom thought he
heard Toby bark. Then a truck driver blasted his
horn. Next Tom thought he saw Toby, but a
light changed at an intersection and traffic began
to move.

A very large parking area surrounded the
coliseum. Mother wound in and out among the
lanes when she was directed to a parking space.
Then came the long walk to the entrance. Mother
left her driving gloves in the station wagon. She
smoothed on fresh white gloves while she clicked
along on her high heels. Tina held her slim neck
stiff as a ruler. Not a hair of her shimmering
page boy swung out of place. Penny pushed one
palm flat to the top of her head to keep her straw

hat in place and tried to keep up with Tina.

Tom watched Terry stump along, not paying much attention to his feet.

"Don't you want Merry to be in the recital?" Tom asked soberly.

Terry grunted, "Sure," but he did not convince Tom. Tom thought maybe Terry did not believe himself.

"Boys, can't you keep up?" Mother asked.

"Aw, Tom is walkin' one step forward and two steps backward," Terry grunted.

Tom was short enough to lose track of his family in the crowd. When Terry paused, Tom hurried to catch up.

Tom was interested in everything he saw: the hundreds and hundreds of cars nosing into parking spaces, the excited parents, the dressed-in-their-best children, the pigeons walking on pink feet in and out among people and cars. Most of all, Tom was interested in a black and white lump he saw near a red roadster. That must be a dog. And if it just happened to be a dog, it might be Toby. Tom's eyes widened with serious interest in the outcome.

Unexpectedly Jim Jackson fell in step with Tom. He answered the question in Tom's eyes. "Parked my bicycle in a rack. Mother brought a carful of neighbors."

"Oh," Tom said. With a swagger of his shoulders, Tom tried to lengthen his stride.

Jim held Tom's hand when they reached the door. Usually Tom did not like to be touched, but this time he was glad to have the tall teenager pull him through the crowd.

Suddenly Tom found himself inside the largest room he had ever seen. In the middle of the floor sat two groups of children. Jim said one group was the band; the other, the orchestra. Although Tom knew how many hundreds of school children sat in those chairs, in the huge room they did not take up much space. Behind the orchestra a chorus sat in bleacher seats. On three walls, bleacher seats for the listeners slanted from the floor almost to the ceiling. So far as Tom could see, every seat was filled.

"Where are we going to sit?" Tom wanted to know.

Father had been watching for his family. He hurried forward and touched Mother's elbow. He guided her back to the seats he had reserved. The Tuckers stayed close to Father, like ducklings on a first swim. Up and up they climbed. Tom's legs were short, and he was glad to accept Jim Jackson's helping hand. Finally they settled in a row of seats high above the orchestra. Tucker knees bumped the shoulders and hat brims of the people who sat ahead. In turn, Tuckers were gouged by the people who sat behind. Cheerful people leaned forward, pointed and counted, locating their own children.

"Where's Merry?" Penny asked as soon as they sat down.

"Second chair, front row, right in front of the

director's stand," Father answered proudly. "See her?"

When Tina helped Penny and Tom to find the director's stand, they smiled happily. Yes, there was Merry.

"She has her number," Tom said.

"And her violin," Penny added. Her sweet voice trembled with excitement.

"She can't find us," Terry declared.

Anxiously Tom looked down into the big, big space. Merry was sitting on the edge of a folding chair. She twisted and craned her neck. She looked at the audience, row by row. Always, when her eyes almost reached the spot where the Tuckers sat, Merry shifted attention to some row ahead of or below her family.

"Oh, dear," Mother said worriedly. "If Merry doesn't find us, she won't be able to play a single note."

"I'll go tell her," Terry offered. Before Father could object, Terry scrambled over feet to the stairs. He clattered, down, down, down to the floor of the auditorium. He walked across the empty space which separated the orchestra from the audience. Merry saw him coming and she stood up.

Merry looked as tiny as a doll, but Tom could see the gladness of her smile. Tom relaxed and grinned up at Jim Jackson.

Terry leaned his head close to Merry's and pointed. When Merry saw her family she waved the violin bow. Then she settled back and arranged her music on the rack. She was ready to work.

Terry hesitated when he reached the middle of the floor. He stared up at the crowd. Then *his* eyes began to search.

"Oh, dear," Mother said, fanning herself with a white handkerchief, "now Terry's lost."

Jim Jackson stood up. "I'll go after him, Mrs. Tucker," he said.

Father grinned when Jim stepped over his

feet. "Better take a compass so *you* won't get lost," he advised with a humorous lift of his black eyebrows.

Anxiously Tom watched a very small Terry walk a long, long way to a wall and lean there, shoulders hunched, hands in pockets. Then Jim walked up to Terry, clapped his shoulder, and guided Terry back up the stairs to the Tucker group.

While Jim and Terry were climbing the aisle stairs, Tom glimpsed a black and white movement close to the floor at the door. Alertly, Tom watched. It could not be a child. It was not the right shape. It had to be—yes, it was. It was Toby.

Unnoticed by the ushers, Toby had entered with some latecomers. The big dog collapsed with his woolly head on his front feet. Tom could see Toby was exhausted from his long, hard run to the coliseum. Tom thought it wise not to call Father's attention to Toby's arrival.

Having located Toby, Tom paid scant attention to the musicians. However, his attention was caught when the master of ceremonies introduced Mr. Jones. Mr. Jones turned his back to the audience. He raised his baton. Suddenly arms began to move, violin strings began to quiver, and sound began to rise. All the violinists looked so much alike that for a moment Tom lost track of Merry.

But not for long. Toby decided to investigate. Toby sat up. He dangled his long red tongue and flopped his curly bangs to peer through beady little eyes. Evidently deciding he should know somebody who made sounds like that, Toby woofed a question. On the bleachers, people jumped. One small boy slid off his seat and reached for Toby.

Toby stepped beyond reach and spoke again. *Louder*. This time more people noticed. They made motions with their hands. The boy quickly followed Toby.

The big dog ran a few steps and reached a spot where he was fully visible from every seat in the audience. The boy's mother stood up, and the boy ran back to his seat.

"Wh-why, Bill, that's Toby!" Mother stammered.

Father cupped a hand around his mouth. He growled at Terry, "Who brought that dog?"

"Nobody brought him," Terry answered in

honest surprise. "He's just here!"

Just then Toby pointed his nose at the ceiling. Toby cried, a thin, lonely cry. The director, Mr. Jones, was standing on a box. He stepped backward and wobbled for balance. Merry half-rose from her chair and forgot to play. Toby saw Merry. He wiggled so happily all his curls bounced. He trotted across the wide empty space.

Terry rose to a crouching position and whispered loudly. "I'll go get Toby."

"There will be a worse commotion if you get into the act. Sit down," Father ordered.

Unwillingly, Terry sat down.

All around the Tucker family group, people whispered behind their programs. It made Tom feel very important, but Tina sat up so straight she curved backward. Her cheeks blazed. Tina, too, kept her eyes on Toby.

The first musical number ended. Tom clapped his hands when the people around him began to applaud with great enthusiasm.

Down in the orchestra, Toby stood up by Merry and tried to lick her face. Merry pushed him back. When Toby crouched with his head hanging down, Tom knew Toby's feelings were hurt.

Mr. Jones made an announcement. He asked the audience to notice the excellence of the vibrato in the next number. The strings of the one hundred and twenty violins and four big cellos began to tremble and cry. So did Toby. He lifted his nose. He opened his big mouth. Toby whimpered mournfully.

"That dog!" Mother scolded. She fanned her face with her white handkerchief.

"Toby's ears hurt," Terry defended Toby.

"He's disturbing everybody," Mother complained.

"Ssh," Father warned. "So are we."

"Oh, dear," Mother mourned. She fanned harder. Tina clenched her hands in her lap. Terry put his elbows on his knees. He propped his chin in his hands while he watched Toby. Out of the side of his mouth Terry muttered, "Guess that will show old Merry it isn't so hot, playing in an orchestra."

Tom scowled at Terry. "That's mean," he told Terry. He forgot to whisper, and the words came out deep and distinct.

Terry turned red and cracked his knuckles.

Beside Tom, Jim Jackson folded his hands across his chest. He stretched his legs till his feet almost touched a fat man's belt. He grinned broadly. Jim told Tom, "I didn't know a recital was such fun."

Tom forgot about Terry. He nodded happily at Jim. "Neither did I," he agreed.

For several minutes Toby lay quietly at Merry's feet.

Mr. Jones told the audience, "We will now play 'Tiptoe.' This is one of our favorites because of the pizzicato effect."

One hundred and twenty grade school violinists began to pluck the strings instead of bowing. Tom settled back, in a very grown-up manner, to enjoy the recital—never dreaming what was about to happen.

6
Crisis on Valley View

Down in the orchestra things began to happen. Toby sat up. He bumped Merry's elbow with his nose. Merry made a loud, clunking sound and swung her whole body. Her violin's neck bumped the elbow of a blond girl with a ponytail. This girl raked three strings with her plucking finger. Furiously she turned on Merry.

Suddenly both girls were tangled in ribbons, numbers, violins, and bows. Sheets of music fell on the floor. The girls ducked to pick up the papers, bumped heads and sat up. They glared, completely forgetful of audience.

A tall, dark boy laid his violin on his chair. With knees bent to make himself shorter, he crept around Merry's chair. When he faced the blond girl, he put his fingers over his lips. Tom knew that boy was saying, "Ssh!"

On his box, Mr. Jones pumped his arms in a fury of directing. The audience began to titter. Merry shoved Toby. Toby bumped the strange boy. Toby barked. Some especially high notes hurt the dog's ears. Toby put back his head. This time he did not whimper—he howled. Long, loudly, mournfully, Toby howled.

A man with a big camera rushed out of the audience. He crouched close to Merry, Toby, the blond girl, and the dark boy. A light flashed when he took a picture.

Terry did not wait for permission to leave his place. He stumbled over feet and found his way to the stair-aisle in the bleachers. Terry clattered down, down, down, not even trying to tiptoe.

Mr. Jones worked harder than ever. Half the orchestra forgot to play. They rose in their chairs to see what was happening. People began to laugh aloud. Mother fanned. Tina's face grew red, then redder. Father pulled a handkerchief from his hip pocket and wiped his forehead.

Terry reached the floor level. He dashed across the wide space and into the orchestra. He took hold of Toby's collar with both hands. Terry pulled. Merry pushed. Toby howled. The blond girl stood up and stamped her feet. The dark boy made "shushing" motions with both hands.

Terry turned such an imploring face to the

audience, Jim Jackson hurried down the stairs to help control Toby.

"Mother," Tina whispered shakily. "That's *twice* Jim has gone down there after Terry."

Drily Father muttered, "The audience knows they're here."

Tom nodded. Father was right. Hundreds and hundreds of heads were turned to watch Merry, Terry, and Toby. That pleased Tom.

Something about that blond girl began to interest Tom. She was not one of Merry's school friends, still she looked familiar. Suddenly Tom hit one palm with a plump fist. That girl was Colin Whitney Blake's cousin. And *that*—that must be Colin Whitney Blake himself picking up scattered music and coaxing the blond girl back to her chair.

Tina was interested in all the Blakes, Tom knew. So he slid along the space Terry and Jim had vacated and leaned across Father's knees. He told Tina, "That's Colin Whitney Blake.

B-l-a-k-e." He looked very proud of himself.

Tina moaned. She put her finger tips on her pink mouth. "Oh, no!" she cried.

"Yep, it is," Tom insisted.

By this time the audience rocked with laughter. Terry and Jim pulled Toby away from Merry's chair and out onto the open floor. Toby braced all four feet and scooted along on feet and tail like a sled on runners. Terry and teenage Jim disappeared through the double entrance doors with Toby. They did not come back for a long, long time. When they did, Jim and Terry sat quietly on the bottom row of the bleachers, near the door.

The dark Blake boy, his blond cousin, and Merry sat down, not looking at each other.

The orchestra finished its program. The band played. Everybody stood up to sing "The Star-Spangled Banner." The folk dancers wore Mexican costumes made of rugs, blankets, and dresser scarves. They hopped and stamped, clapped hands and jerked at their costumes.

Only Father and Tom enjoyed the program. Father grinned broadly and patted Mother's hand. After a while Mother smiled mistily. She stopped fanning her face.

Penny patted Tina's hand. But Tina was not to be comforted—she looked ready to explode in little pieces.

The last handclap died away. The audience began to move along the bleachers and down the aisle-stairs. Tina moaned, "*Why* did it have to be the Blake boy? He will *hate* us."

"He doesn't even know you," Father reminded her, looking puzzled.

"He knows Merry," Tina mourned.

In spite of all interruptions, the recital was well received by an indulgent audience of parents and friends. And, Merry had her picture in the paper.

At 222 Valley View the next morning, Tom was up first. He carried the paper to the kitchen

and spread it below the big window to look at
the pictures. Tom found a picture of a zoo ele-
phant trying to cool its feet in a drinking
trough. He studied that scene carefully and
wondered if the trough broke. Then he found a
new picture of Senator Blake. In the middle of
a group, the senator was shaking hands with an
Indian. Everybody, even the senator, wore
feathered headdresses. Tom reminded himself
to cut out that picture after the family read the
paper. Then—there was Merry!

"W—ow!" Tom said softly. "And Toby, too."
Happily Tom studied the picture of Merry.
Scowling fiercely, Merry sawed with her violin
bow while Toby howled in her right ear. The
elbow close to Merry's left ear belonged to Colin
Whitney Blake's girl cousin. The hand on Toby's
collar belonged to Colin Whitney Blake himself.
Right that minute Tom decided to make a scrapbook of his clippings. Merry's picture belonged
on the first page!

Neatly Tom refolded the paper the way Father liked it. Then he trotted barefoot up the stairs to the bedroom shared by Mother and Father. Both were awake. They called, "Good morning!" before Tom reached the door.

"What's the news?" Father asked good-naturedly. He yawned and stretched up his arms to bump the headboard of the double bed.

"Guess," Tom urged.

"City Hall burned down," Father returned promptly.

Tom shook his head.

"An airplane crash?" Mother asked.

Again Tom shook his head.

Terry proved he was awake by shouting, "Did Lake Annabelle dry up and blow away?"

"No!" Tom shouted back. He was unable to keep his secret. He handed the morning paper to Father. Tom told Father, "Turn the pages till I say stop."

Father teased by turning the sheets very

slowly. "This one?" he asked each time he turned. Each time Tom answered, "Keep going." When Father reached page five Tom did not have time to say, "Stop." Father burst out, "Blow me down!" which was one of Grandfather Tucker's sayings.

Mother sat up and tugged a margin of the paper. "Bill, let me see, too," she insisted. Then Mother gasped, "Wh-why, it's Merry!"

"Huh? What's Merry?" Terry shouted. He bounded through the door and landed on a side of the bed.

Terry made so much noise, doors opened at the end of the hall. Tina, Merry, and Penny pattered past the sewing room and into the bedroom. Father held the paper high enough for everybody to see the picture of Merry.

Penny bounced in a ring-dance with Merry. Terry crowed, "Good old Toby got his picture in the paper!" Tom smiled at everybody.

But Tina's face crumpled. "Oh, that's an

awful disgrace!" she wailed.

Drily Father reminded her, "I thought you wanted Merry's picture in the paper, Tina."

"Not with Toby howling in her ear!" Tina flung back.

Grinning broadly, Terry said, "Bet that was old Toby's highest note."

Father raised his dark eyebrows and pursed his lips. "Probably," he agreed. "Toby's nose seems to be tilted at the correct angle for a real ceiling raiser."

"Father, how can you laugh?" Tina demanded. "*Everybody* reads the paper. People will *laugh* at Merry."

Father's face sobered. "Why should you care, Tina, if Merry doesn't?"

"She cares," Tina rattled. "You do care, don't you, Merry?"

Merry and Penny stopped prancing. They fell in a heap on the foot of the bed. Dark tufts of hair stuck out of Merry's thick braids like straw bursting through a scarecrow's seam. Her eyes twinkled back at Tina. "Nope," she denied cheerfully. "This is the first time I ever had my picture in the paper. I think it's fun."

Tina looked so stricken, Tom tried to comfort her. "I found a picture of the senator. Shall I cut it out for you?"

"Not for me!" Tina flared. "If I—I mean, if *we* ever meet that Blake boy he will laugh at us. Oh!" Tina ran from the room. Almost at once Tom heard her door slam.

Father turned a blank face to Mother. "What brought that on?" he asked.

"Tina has a case of hero worship," Mother said. Her lips smiled, but her eyes didn't. Her eyes looked sad about something, Tom thought.

Father shrugged. "That isn't contagious," he said cheerfully.

Mother looked from Merry to Terry. "I hope not," she told Father.

After breakfast Tom pasted his clippings on

sheets of red construction paper. He carried his papers to the attic to borrow Terry's stapler. Carefully Tom put his book together. Then he carried it to Tina who was in the porch swing with Sugar on her lap. Tina waved Tom away and did not look up from her new book.

"Are the clippings mine now?" Tom asked Tina.

"The clippings are yours now," Tina mumbled, and turned another page.

Tom grunted with satisfaction. He trotted through the front hall and into the kitchen. Mother was working a crossword puzzle while her green apple pies baked. Tom stood beside her and examined the puzzle to see if Mother was punching holes in the picture of the senator with the feathers in his hair. She wasn't.

Mother became aware of Tom. She said, "Oh, you want your clippings now."

"When you finish your puzzle," Tom said patiently.

Mother scrambled through the sheets and found the senator and Merry. She handed them to Tom. He rummaged a cupboard drawer for scissors and bit his tongue while he clipped along the black lines. The picture of the senator went into the middle of his book, but Merry's picture went on the first page, just as he had planned.

When the oven bell rang, Mother rose from the kitchen table to take her pies from the oven. She told Tom, "That's a lovely book."

Tom nodded with satisfaction. "Where shall I keep it?" he asked Mother.

"In your dresser drawer?" she suggested.

Tom objected, "Terry might find it."

"How about the window seat in the study?"

"I like that hiding place," Tom agreed at once. "I won't have to climb the stairs when I want to look at my pictures." He trotted off to store the book he had made.

Merry had been tired before the recital, and was listless all day. After her romp with Penny,

Merry put away the things she had carried home from school. Then she designed paper doll clothes for Penny to color.

Penny was not as strong as the rest of the healthy Tucker clan. It surprised no one when Penny spent hours with paper dolls. Not so with Merry. Everybody who came in sight of the corner window seat in the living room asked, "Are you sick, Merry? Don't you feel well?" Each time Merry answered, "Oh, I'm all right," but nobody believed her. Throughout the day fingers touched Merry's forehead to see if she had a fever. Finally Mother started toward the telephone. "I'm going to call the doctor," she declared. "When Merry sits, she's sick."

"No, Mother," Merry objected. "I'm just tired."

"Or embarrassed," Tina said shrewdly. "If my picture had been in the paper with Toby ruining the recital, I'd hide in the house all day, too, you bet."

"I'm not hiding!" Merry flared. "And I like my picture in the paper."

"Well, I don't," Tina shot back.

"Girls, girls," Father said mildly. He put down the evening newspaper and stretched long legs to rest his heels on a hassock.

"Father looks like a bridge over the Blue River," Penny said giggling.

"River. Lake." Father snapped his fingers and sat up straight. "That is just the cure Merry needs. It's the only answer."

Merry grinned and wrinkled her nose at Father. "Drowning will cure anything," she declared.

"A few days in the cottage on Lake Annabelle is what I have in mind," Father said.

Terry came into the front hall in time to overhear Father's statement. "Hey, I'll buy that," Terry called. "When do we leave?"

"How soon can you be ready?" Father asked. "When the store closes tomorrow?"

"Betcha, boy," Terry crowed. "Wait'll I spread the news!"

Almost at once all the Tuckers, including Mother, gathered around Father's chair in the living room for a "planning bee."

"You can stay at the lake as long as you like," Father promised. "If Grandma wants to go, your grandfather and I can drive out at night, as usual."

Merry brightened. "Are Grandpa and Grandma back from the buying trip?"

"They will be home tomorrow," Father answered. The Tuckers, father and son, owned Tuckers' Town Talk, a variety store on the square at city-center. Grandpa and Grandma had been in Chicago placing their order for Christmas toys and games, so they had missed the grade school recital.

"What are we waiting for?" Merry asked brightly. "Let's go pack."

7
On the Wrong Foot— Again

At midnight the telephone rang. Merry heard it. Sleepily she stumbled down the hall to wake Father. His glad shout, "Hello, Mother!" brought Lois Tucker and all the children to the landing. They hung over the banister to listen to the one-sided conversation. Grandma Tucker's voice sounded sweet and thin when Father tilted the receiver toward the listeners.

Penny ran down the steps to the hall. She begged, "Let me say hello to Grandma please, Father!"

"Me, too!" clamored Terry, Merry, Tina, and Tom. They crowded around the telephone, all shouting at once.

Penny talked first, so Tom was allowed to cradle the telephone. Indian file, the Tuckers started to climb the front stairs. Abruptly Tom turned. "We didn't ask Grandpa for the cottage," he reminded them.

"Hey, that's right!" Terry agreed. All the Tuckers looked at Tom with respect. Tom could always be depended to think to the root of a problem.

"Grandma will say yes," Merry said with confidence.

Grandma said yes, just as Merry had predicted. She even agreed to keep Mother company for as long as the Tuckers wanted to stay at the lake.

"That will be till school starts," Terry declared.

"Or until something more interesting comes along," Father amended Terry's words with a knowing grin.

The next morning every bedroom door burst

open the minute Father's alarm rang. Busily
they raced from four bedrooms to two bathrooms
and to the kitchen. The whole family shouted
suggestions and reminders.

Tom appeared at the breakfast table in bathing trunks. He carried his clipping book with
Merry's picture on the cover.

"We can't go until after store hours," Merry
told Tom.

"Then I'll be ready," Tom retorted.

All day the Tuckers piled heaps of clothing,
books, and games on beds. Tina helped Mother
prepare a picnic supper. They would eat the
food under cottonwoods on the beach. In the late
afternoon, Father rolled into the driveway. Behind him drove Grandpa and Grandma. Mother
and all the children were sitting on the front
porch surrounded by bags and boxes. "All
aboard!" Father shouted.

Terry ran to open the double doors of the old
coach house at the end of the lot. He hopped

like corn in a popper while Father hitched the old vacation trailer to the station wagon. The trailer would serve as a summer bedroom for Mother and the girls. Tom hooked his thumbs in the elastic band of his red bathing trunks. He watched Father lock the trailer hitch. "Okay?" Father asked. He, too, studied the locked trailer hitch.

"Okay," Tom approved.

Within a few minutes both Grandpa's sedan and Father's station wagon were loaded with Tuckers, food, and pets. Merry forgot she was tired. Now that the recital was past, Terry dropped his jealousy into a dark corner of his mind. He bantered with Merry and Tom. Penny sat between Mother and Father in the front seat. She squealed when she recognized familiar landmarks.

Tina relaxed for the first time since Merry's picture had appeared. She did not object to sitting between Toby and Sugar, even when Toby "sat tall" and breathed down her neck. Once Tina saw a boy on a motor scooter. He looked so much like the Blake boy, her cheeks burned. Thank goodness, she was going to the lake, where she could forget about those Blakes.

The next morning roly-poly, white-haired Grandma served an early breakfast in the cottage. Grandpa and Father left for their days' work at Tuckers' Town Talk. Mother organized the settling-in activity. Long before noon the cabin was in order.

As soon as they were free, the five young Tuckers raced up Grandpa's private road to the highway to meet Mr. Wilson, the milkman. Each tried to win the race to tell him they were customers again.

When they reached the intersection, the highway was empty. After a wait of several minutes only a couple of cars and a pickup rolled past. "Maybe we have missed the milkman," Merry suggested. "He might have been early."

Tom saw a patch of white in a strong wooden box nailed to a tree. "Somebody left a note for Mr. Wilson, I'll betcha," he suggested shrewdly.

Terry loped across a grassy space. He reached for the note.

Tina asked sharply, "Terry, should you read other people's mail?"

"This isn't mail," Terry retorted. "It's just Anne Green's order for the milkman, and it isn't sealed."

"It isn't in an envelope or in a mailbox," Tom pointed out.

"All it says is, 'Please leave four quarts of milk Saturday morning,' " Terry said. He shot a teasing, got-ahead-of-you grin at Tina. He put the note back in the box.

"This is Saturday," Tom rumbled. "So Mr. Wilson hasn't come by yet. The note's still there!"

"Hopscotch?" Merry shouted.

The five scrambled for odd-shaped pebbles to toss. Terry dug a hopscotch court on the ground with a stick. While they waited for Mr. Wilson's truck, they tossed and hopped, turned, tossed and hopped again. Several maples surrounded the shaded clearing. The Tuckers had played here many times while waiting for the milkman or mailman. It did not occur to any of the children to be watchful.

Penny hopped up the squares. She balanced

on one foot to recover her white pebble. When she straightened, Penny squealed excitedly. She tottered.

"You touched," Tom accused.

Penny paid no attention to either Tom or the game. "L-Look!" she stammered. A trembling finger pointed at a clump of bushes beside a path through the woods.

The rest of the Tuckers moved closer to each other and to Penny while they looked. Then Terry said disgustedly, "Aw, look, it's only a cow!"

"Not just *a* cow," Merry corrected. "Lots of cows!"

Almost at once several cows pushed through the bushes. They blinked at their unexpected encounter with human beings. The animals took a few uncertain steps. Then they followed a placid-looking red cow onto the highway. Other cattle came out of the woods. They crossed the clearing and bunched on the highway.

"H-How many of them are there?" Penny quavered.

"Where do they belong?" Tina wondered.

The last cow to come out of the woods was a large black animal. Her high hipbones were marked with ovals of white. "Now I know who owns those cows!" Terry said with a deep sigh of relief. "That's Old Owly. She belongs to the Coopers."

"Old Owly?" Penny repeated.

"Because of the white spots. They look like owl's eyes," Terry explained.

A red car came around the curve, closely followed by the milk truck. The cattle milled in a confused mass. The red car could barely creep. Mr. Wilson stopped near Tom. "Hello, Tuckers, welcome back!" he called cheerfully. "Need any milk today?"

With a swagger of importance, Tom gave Mr. Wilson Grandma's order. Then he moved away from the wheels while the truck pushed among the cattle. "We should drive those cows back to their pasture," Tom said soberly.

"Good idea!" Terry agreed. He snatched up a stick and darted toward Old Owly. He flourished the stick and screeched. The cow blinked. She swung her head. Then she decided to keep away from contact with the stick. She lumbered back into the clearing at the side of the road.

The rest of the Tuckers picked up sticks. They whooped along at the heels of the cattle to drive them home.

Terry knew where the path joined the lane to the Cooper farm. The Tuckers urged the cattle into a swinging trot. They herded them through the long, winding lane and into a pleasant pasture. Terry closed and Tom fastened the gate. Then the children paused to see exactly where they were.

"I can see the lake," Penny said. Her thin face lighted with pleasure.

"Betcha that's our brook," Tom said. He pointed at a brook which flowed under brush and trees through the middle of a sloping meadow. At the bottom of the slope a strip of young trees separated Lake Annabelle from the farm. Merry found the roof of Anne Green's cottage among the trees, but Grandpa's property was hidden.

"Betcha you're right," Terry agreed. "This brook runs into the lake on the south side of our sand bar."

Merry spun on her heel. She shouted, "Last one to the sand bar is a creepy snail!" Merry darted back up the farm lane. The rest of the Tuckers gave instant chase.

They ran till Penny began to wheeze. Then they slowed down, but nobody minded. The cattle's hooves had beaten the ruts of the lane into deep, fine dust. "I like hot dirt," Tom declared happily. He jumped. Dust rose higher. Terry jumped and spattered dust as high as his belt. Fluffy clouds billowed around his feet.

Tom sat beside the lane and unstrapped his sandals.

"What do you think you're doing, Tom?" Terry asked.

"I'm going to jump barefoot," Tom retorted. When he was most excited, Tom's face was sober. Now he did not crack a smile, but his ears reddened.

"Hey!" Terry shouted. "That's a super idea. Let's dust-wade!"

Instantly all the rest of the Tuckers perched beside the Cooper lane like crows on a limb. They took off sandals and sneakers and stuffed them in pockets and belts.

Noisily they jumped and splashed in the hot dust. Perspiration streaks on faces became tiny rivers of mud. Dust settled into neck creases like wire necklaces. Shrieking with laughter, they forgot other people existed. The Tuckers were having fun.

They reached the highway just as a motor
scooter came around the curve—and the driver
was Colin Whitney Blake!

Merry was leading the Tucker parade. She
clapped both dusty hands over her mouth and
squealed. Her eyes searched. Not a bush or a
tree grew close enough to duck behind before she
was recognized. She glimpsed Tina diving into
a clump of young cedars. "Wait for me!" Merry
shrieked.

Merry dived at Tina's heels, but it was too
late.

"Hello Merry Tucker," called Colin Whitney
Blake. He lifted one clean hand in a cheerful
greeting.

With a sheepish grin Merry waggled dirty
fingers at the neatly dressed Blake boy. While
she picked pieces of cedar needles out of her
braids, she edged forward.

The spotless collar of a checked gingham shirt
lay over the boy's jacket lapels. The crease of his

slacks was a sharp line. Merry twisted one bare
foot behind an ankle. Ugh! Why had she jumped
in that dirt?

Before Merry could choke out a greeting, Toby
bounced into the highway. He barked an excited
welcome. The Blake boy dodged. Dust spurted up
from the wheels of his motor scooter. From the
cedar clump Tina moaned, "Oh, that dog!"

Toby thought he recognized a game. Wildly
barking, he bounced in curl-waving excitement.
Toby circled the motor scooter. The Blake boy
zigged, and then he zagged. He came to a wob-
bling stop just short of a tree at the edge of the
road.

Anxiously Merry ran forward. "H-Hullo," she
stammered. "Are you hurt?"

The boy slapped at his perfectly pressed slacks.
Then he brushed a jacket sleeve which Toby had
pawed. Looking lean and older than his eleven
years, the boy smiled. "I think I'll live," he
admitted. He patted the top of Toby's big head.

Toby waggled and dangled his red tongue. "I thought I recognized your dog," the Blake boy said, grinning.

Terry stepped forward, scowling. "What's wrong with our dog anyway?" he demanded grumpily.

"Nothing," Colin Whitney Blake said, sounding surprised.

Terry's lower lip did not go back into place. Quickly Merry said, "This is my twin brother, Terry."

Politely the boy nodded and said, "We've met before."

Merry was overcome with admiration for his grown-up manner. She almost forgot to introduce the rest of her family. Penny nudged Merry's arm. Merry glanced down at her smaller sister, and stammered when she noticed Penny's smeared, dirty face. Penny was the one member of the Tucker family who could be counted on to appear clean and pretty. Oh! Even Penny was a mess. What must this senator's son be thinking of the Tuckers? "Th-this is P-Penny," Merry said feebly.

Penny smiled sunnily.

Tom trotted forward. "Hullo, Colin Whitney Blake," Tom said, rumbling the words from the bottom of his throat. "I know you. I saw your picture."

The Blake boy shook hands with Tom. When the handclasp was completed, he wiped his right hand with a clean handkerchief. "My name is Whitney," he told Tom.

Tom's unsmiling blue eyes, examined Whitney Blake from the top of his dark head to his doeskin oxfords. Then he turned and trotted back to the cedars. "Tina," Tom said clearly and distinctly, "come out. You can see Colin Whitney Blake. He's talking to Merry."

"I—I know." Tina emerged from the cedars. She blushed with confusion and refused to fol-low Tom. She shot a beseeching oh-please-skip-

me glance at Merry, which Merry pretended not
to see.

"This is Tina," Merry said. "She's in sixth
grade and she plays piano."

Alertly Whitney looked at Tina. "Perhaps we
could practice together sometime," he suggested.
"I play violin."

"I know," Tom interrupted. "I was at the
recital. I saw you."

The Blake boy colored, but he grinned. "Everybody saw me," he admitted.

"That was because of Toby," Tom said
happily. He bobbed his head while he recalled
the evening which had put Toby so much in the
limelight.

A silence fell. Whitney Blake waited for somebody to speak. Then he said, "This is what I
thought your family would be like, Merry."

Terry scowled more fiercely than ever. He
bumped the ground with a bare heel. He wished
contact with Colin Whitney Blake did not always

put Terry Tucker in a bad light. Out of the side of his mouth Terry muttered to Tom, "So old Whit thought we would be a bunch of dirty slobs, huh?"

Tom paid no attention to Terry. He invited Whitney, "Come play? We've been jumping in the dirt."

The boy laughed aloud, and Merry giggled.

Tina did not giggle. She took a step backward toward the cedars. She pulled Tom with her.

Through clenched teeth she muttered, "Tom, don't you *dare* say another word."

Tom did not speak with his tongue, but his eyes accused Tina of unfriendliness.

Whitney Blake hesitated. He glanced down the dirt lane. Then he mumbled an excuse and putt-putted down the highway.

Five silent Tuckers watched him round the curve near the mailboxes. They turned toward the head of Grandpa's private road. Merry made a determined effort to skip, but Tina glowered at her.

Toby walked close to Tina. He pushed his cold nose into the palm of one of her stiffly swinging arms. "Go 'way," she ordered coldly. "All you do is embarrass us."

"Toby didn't 'barrass me," Tom insisted sturdily.

Tenderhearted Penny put a thin, protective arm across the big dog's shoulders. She walked beside Toby, even when he tried to make side-trips on rabbit trails. "Usually Toby behaves," Penny pleaded with Tina. "Usually he is a good dog."

But Tina just scowled.

8
Dream World
Made Real

By the time the hot, dust-smeared Tuckers reached Grandpa's cottage, everybody but Tina had shrugged off the meeting with Whitney Blake. Even Tina told herself, "Oh, well, I'll never see him again."

Clumsy as a bear cub, Terry clapped Merry's shoulder. "Swim?" he invited.

"Sure," she responded instantly.

Merry and Penny, followed by Tina, hurried into the vacation trailer to put on their bathing suits. The boys ran to the sleeping porch to change. "Bring back your dirty clothes," Tina called.

The four younger Tuckers flung their dusty

clothes in the general direction of the kitchen door as they raced to the beach. Tina stopped long enough to load the automatic washer. While she measured soap, she heard voices in the living room. Anne Green, whose beach home was Green Fields, was talking to Mother and Grandma. Tina heard her say, "I don't dare leave the baby out in his carriage to sun."

"Oh?" Mother made a questioning sound.

Tina could think of no reason why a baby would not be safe on the quiet shores of Lake Annabelle.

"I never know when a huge cow will step out of the bushes," Anne declared, sounding annoyed. "Every time I go for the mail or milk or to walk the baby, I have to watch out for cattle. The place is simply overrun with the pesky animals."

Tina heard Grandma chirp, "It's against the law to allow cattle to run free. Do you know who owns the animals?"

Anne Green answered, "My husband says they

belong to Mr. Cooper, but the man is in the hospital. His wife and children are trying to keep the farm going. Somebody is failing to lock the pasture gate."

"I'm sure the cows aren't dangerous," Grandma soothed.

"I hope not!" Anne declared with feeling. "I'm a city gal myself. Cows bother me."

Tina set the dial of the washer. She ran barefoot down the shaded path to the beach. At the spots where brush and young trees made an arbor over the path, Tina slowed. Her heart thumped, even while common sense told her no cow was going to charge out of nowhere. After all, the rest of the children had gone down the path with perfect safety. She could hear them yelling at each other. With a burst of speed, Tina shot out of the path and onto the beach.

Tom was running for a beachball thrown by Penny. He dodged out of Tina's way. "Something chasing you?" he asked with interest.

"No," Tina answered briefly. But she glanced over her shoulder to be sure. Even though Uncle Fred owned a dairy farm in the northern part of the state, Tina, too, was a city gal. Cows bothered her.

At supper that night Mother reported what Anne Green had said about the cows.

"We drove those cows home," Tom said.

"You didn't!" Mother exclaimed anxiously.

Father listened carefully while the children told their story of driving the cattle back to the Cooper farm. "Was the bull out of his pen?" Father asked.

"No, sir, just cows," Tom said positively.

"Then I'm sure you are safe to walk where you choose," Father told Mother. "If you see the cattle, it might be a good idea to telephone the Coopers to come after them." Father drained his coffee cup. He patted his mouth with his napkin and pushed back his chair. "Who's for a boat ride?" he asked cheerfully.

Hands raised. Voices shouted, "I! I!"

"Mother? Dad?" Father asked Grandma and Grandpa.

"It's a pleasant evening. I'm going to sit in the yard until the mosquitoes drive me in," Grandpa declared.

"I'll sit with you, dear," Grandma told him.

While Father filled the gasoline tank, Tom dusted the seats of Grandpa's boat, the Tub. Grandpa had been in the Navy in his youth, and he believed in safety, not speed. The Tub was large enough to hold the whole family and Toby in its banana-shaped hull. It was solid enough to reassure Grandma, who was afraid of water.

Mother and the three girls were last to reach the dock. Mother nodded and smiled while Father placed each child in exactly the right spot to balance the load. Then she accepted his help and took the seat in the prow.

The Tuckers waved and shouted to Grandma

and Grandpa who were already comfortably settled in the front yard. Insect flares burned near their chairs. "A mosquito won't dare get close to Grandpa," Penny declared happily.

"Whither away?" Father asked when the Tub pulled away from dock.

"Who cares?" Mother asked gaily.

Tina cared. Suddenly she cared very much. She wanted to see the house Senator Blake had copied from a palatial residence in Venice. She wanted to see where Whitney Blake lived. She dampened her lips with her tongue, but she could not say the words aloud. Tina was glad when Merry piped, "Why don't we go straight to the end of the lake and back?"

"Yeah," Terry agreed with his twin. "We can explore our end of the lake by ourselves. Let's see something different!"

Father sounded doubtful. "We may not have enough gas. The can wasn't full."

Penny made a little murmur of disappointment. The others echoed her.

Quickly Tom reminded them, "We have oars."

"So we have," Father agreed good-naturedly. "And six pairs of strong arms to take turn-about with the rowing."

"You left out somebody," Tom declared.

"Father didn't count me," Penny told Tom. "He thinks I'm not strong enough."

"I'm strong enough," Tom said sturdily. "I'm strong enough for anything."

"Anything your size," Mother corrected.

Tina heard, and she saw. She even spoke when she was spoken to, but her mind was not on the present moment. She made up a scene of her own, with its own special time and place. The hero was a tall, lean young man with a boy's face. He was on the horse she had seen in the newspaper clipping. He was smiling at the girl who rode beside him.

Father guided the Tub in and out, following the shoreline. While she watched the familiar scenes, Tina gathered courage to place herself on that second horse. She wore her hair in a ponytail. A mass of perfect blond curls lay high on her forehead. And, oh, she was so beautiful the boy turned to look at her.

No embarrassment touched Tina's dream world; no barking dogs, no upset recital, no ridiculous picture in the paper, no dust smears, no talkative brothers and sisters. Some place in the background strode a broad-chested senator wearing—Tina hesitated. Did senators wear long black robes, or was she thinking of a judge?

Momentarily jarred out of her fantasy, Tina saw that Father had reached the end of the lake. This bay was lined with homes of the wealthy and influential.

Father whistled and said, "We'd have to sell our house to buy a boat like that."

Tina turned her blond head to examine a boat which cost as much as the comfortable old house at 222 Valley View. The boat was blue and white, long, sleek and powerful. Its name was Lady. The Lady was moored at a dock which seemed to protrude from a high cement sea wall. In the gathering dusk, Tina raised her eyes to the top of the wall. With a start of surprise she realized this was no sea wall.

She was looking at the basement wall of a house built, not above or beside, but in the water. Triangular flags fluttered from poles on bulky twin towers. Bumpy red tiles roofed the large house. Tina almost expected an imprisoned princess to peep through one of the tall, leaded windows. Why, this was Senator Blake's Lake Annabelle home!

And *that* was Senator Blake's son on the dock.

Tina gulped with surprise. She twisted her long, slim fingers into a knot. Shyly she watched Whitney Blake trot down the dock to the end of a high diving board.

The boy paused briefly. He flexed muscles and gathered power. Then he darted to the end of the board. He jumped hard and high on the canvas padding and shot upward. He doubled in a perfect jackknife, straightened, and entered the water like an arrow. The boy surfaced several feet from the dock. He shook water from dark hair and eyes, and swam to the dock ladder. His crawl stroke was so perfect it looked easy.

Whitney Blake climbed the ladder. He walked foward toward the diving board, leaving a trail of water-drips.

"Oh, boy," Tom boomed in his big voice. "Maybe he will do that again."

Maybe he will, whispered Tina's heart.

At just that moment the motor of the Tub coughed. It gave up.

"Out of gas," Father said. He sounded slightly I-told-you-so.

"Oh, no," Tina moaned under her breath. "Not here. Not in front of Whitney Blake."

Tina's frantic hope that Whitney Blake might not see the Tub was not realized. Whitney turned his head when the motor barked. He lifted a hand in greeting. Evidently recognizing the Tuckers, he waved and beckoned.

"That's Colin Whitney Blake," Tom declared in his carrying voice.

"Oh! Oh, no!" Tina moaned aloud. "Why are we always in a mess when that boy sees us?"

Father seemed interested in Tom's statement. He turned to look at the boy on the dock. "Maybe he can loan us a can of gas," Father said hope-

fully. "Otherwise, we're out of luck."

"Oh, Father, you wouldn't ask him!" Tina pleaded.

"It's a long row home," Father answered drily. "I'll put my pride in my pocket. Why shouldn't I ask him?"

"He—he's a *senator's* son," Tina said close to tears.

"What kind of a reason is that?" Terry demanded.

To Tina, it was the strongest reason in the world. She did not want her family placed in uncomplimentary contrast with the hero of her dream. Most of all, she did not want to step out of that dream to be recognized herself.

Before Tina could choke down this new embarrassment, Tom boomed across the quiet water, "Hi, Colin Whitney Blake, do you have some gas we can borrow?"

Tina shook Tom's shoulder. "We don't call people by their full names," she scolded.

"Why not?" Tom wanted to know. His voice deepened and grew in volume. "That's his name, isn't it? Colin Whitney Blake. B-l-a-k-e."

"Oh!" Tina wailed helplessly. She cringed in her seat and twisted her fingers.

Father traded places with the twins in the middle seat. He put the oars in the oarlocks and rowed to the dock. Wiggling dark shadows slithered along the edges of the water disturbed by the oars. The dusk-call of doves floated down from the twin towers. Up in that imposing house somebody laughed.

When the Tub nosed the edge of the dock, Whitney Blake reached out a hand to guide the boat into position beside the dock ladder. He sat on heels to steady the Tub.

Merry chirped happily, "Are we glad to see you! Whitney, this is my mother, and this is my father. We—"

Tina nudged Merry between her shoulder blades. She whispered fiercely, "Merry, you

know we're supposed to introduce children to
grownups!"

Merry swung her dark braids. She asked flip-
pantly, "What difference does it make? Now
they know each other's names."

"He will think we don't have any manners at
all," Tina scolded in a whisper. She drew a deep,
trembling breath and turned her attention to
Father. Without knowing her dream world
existed, her whole family seemed determined to
break it in little pieces. Tina shivered while she
waited for Father to add further embarrassment.

To her relief, Father's attitude toward Whitney Blake was man-to-man. Father explained
about the gasoline. It was now too dark to see
Father's expression, but his voice sounded
relaxed and humorous. "Guess I thought I could
go home on fumes," Father said.

The Blake boy chuckled. "I've had the same
experience," he admitted.

"In that blue boat?" Tom boomed.

The boy turned to look down into the Tub. "In that blue boat," he told Tom.

"Betcha that boat's hard to row," Tom decided, after a considering pause. Tom's best friend was teen-age Jim Jackson. It was not hard for him to talk to older boys. Tina almost envied Tom the sureness inside himself. To Tom, people were people, and he liked them. He was sure they liked him, too.

"It isn't easy with one paddle," Whitney Blake retorted, chuckling.

Tina liked the sound of the boy's easy chuckle.

The boy loped down the dock. He bent his elbows at his sides like a distance runner. He went through a door Tina had failed to notice in the cement basement wall. Almost at once Whitney returned with a red gasoline can and funnel. He gave them to Father.

Terry clung to the edge of the dock. It was an unnecessary waste of energy, since the Blake boy sat on his heels to steady the Tub for Father. Gasoline gurgled through the funnel into Grandpa's gas tank. The odor was clean but nose-tickling.

Father stood up and gave Whitney Blake the can and funnel. "Thanks," he said heartily. "We'll return your gas tomorrow."

"My pleasure," the boy answered easily.

Tom made a sound. Tina poked him in the back, knowing Tom was going to ask the boy what he meant. That simply must not happen! Already the boy must consider the Tuckers an unmannerly, messy family. He must not think they could not understand the English language.

Father pulled away from the dock, maneuvering carefully in the dim light. Then Tom twisted to face Tina. "Well?" he demanded. "What did Colin Whitney Blake mean?"

Father answered for Tina. "He meant we don't have to bring back the gas."

"Why didn't he say so?" Terry asked sourly.

From the prow seat Mother spoke, soothing ruffled feelings with her sweet, cheerful voice. "Probably he hears his father use the phrase," she explained.

All eyes turned toward Father, a dark blob in the fading light. Each Tucker compared him with the senator no Tucker had met. Not one of them had ever heard Father say, "My pleasure."

Father asked with relaxed good humor, "Well? Do I pass inspection, or are you five going to trade me in for a senator?"

"We like you the way you are," Penny insisted. She sounded so sober, the rest of the family laughed.

The tension was broken, but Tina could not walk back into her dream world. She kept remembering the friendliness and helpfulness of the real boy.

9
Another Boat Ride

The next day was Sunday. A dozen times Tina suggested that Father drive down the highway to a station for a can of gasoline. A dozen times Father put her off with an excuse.

"My pleasure. Remember?" Tom reminded Tina.

Almost crossly Tina retorted, "It is *my* pleasure to return that can of gas. We can't be obligated to a senator. We simply can't!"

Father agreed, but not for the same reason. He did not bring the gasoline until he returned from work Monday. Tina was waiting for him in Grandpa's parking lot. "Did you bring it?" she demanded.

Father pretended not to understand. "The new magazines?" he countered. "Here they are. You can take them to Mother while I carry the groceries."

"The gas!" Tina insisted impatiently.

"Oh, that," Father said, shrugging. "Yes. I brought it."

"Good." Tina sounded so breathless, Father turned for an examination of her face. Tina flushed and hurried down the path to the back door with the roll of new magazines. She did not know what Father read in her face.

Tina was already gathering up water-safety belts when Father entered the kitchen. He slid the large box of groceries onto the end of a counter. "What's the hurry, Tina?" Father asked. "Give me time. I'm bushed. This was freight day at the store, you know."

"You don't have to go, Father. We could go to the end of the lake and back by ourselves." Tina stopped to catch her breath. She knew she was talking too fast, and she did not know how to stop.

"I'll talk it over with your mother," Father said. Tiredly he rubbed the back of his neck while he stared through a window at the glassy surface of Lake Annabelle.

Mother entered from the living room. She linked an arm through Father's and leaned her cheek against his sleeve. "What are we discussing, Bill?" she asked.

"Whether or not to allow the kids to take the boat to the Blake house tonight," Father told her.

"Isn't it a bit late to let the children take the boat?" Uneasily Mother scanned the lake.

"There's no wind!" Tina pleaded. "And we'll be very careful."

Tina thought the silence which followed would never break. Then Mother asked, "What do you think, Bill?"

"There's no wind," Father said, "They can't get lost, even if they return after dark. I'll turn on the dock light. No matter how confused they become, they can reach home safely by following the shoreline."

Tina knew the matter was settled, even before Mother said, "Yes." She darted out of the kitchen and into the yard. She cupped her hands and shouted, "Boat ride!"

Tom was combing Toby's long curls. Merry and Terry pitched horseshoes. Penny lay on her stomach on a blanket while she designed paper-

doll clothes. All four stopped what they were doing and ran.

"Where?" Merry shouted.

"Alone?" Terry wanted to know. The racing twins slid to a halt beside Tina.

"All alone. All the way to the Blake house," Tina said dramatically.

The Tuckers began to glow at the idea of a night-ride without an adult in the boat. This was an adventure.

Father and Mother joined the excited children. "Maybe the little ones had better not go," Mother said anxiously.

Tom pushed out his lower lip. "Who's little?" he demanded. "I weigh more than Penny."

"I'm taller than Tom!" Penny declared. She stretched her thin body to full height.

"Okay, okay," Father said, chuckling. "We get the point. There are no *little* Tuckers."

"Younger," Tom said in his Grandpa voice.

"But not littler," Penny declared.

While Mother and Grandma put the simple evening meal on the big kitchen table, Tina locked herself in the bathroom. She combed her hair three times. Then she hurried to the trailer to change her playsuit twice. Even then Tina was not pleased with her appearance.

Merry was scowling when she jerked open the trailer door and joined Tina. "Father sent me to change my blouse before supper," she announced.

"I should think so," Tina scolded. "You need clean shorts, too."

"What's the matter with the shorts I have on?" Merry demanded. She put hands on hips and dared Tina to criticize.

"They're the wrong color for any of your blouses," Tina said coolly. "You just can't wear plaid pants and a flowered blouse in public."

"What's public about a boat ride?" Merry shot back in honest surprise.

"We're going to the Blakes'!" Tina raised her

voice when she realized her cheeks were getting hot.

"To their dock," Merry reminded. "To return a can of gas."

Merry scrambled through all the clothes in her suitcase. She found nothing that pleased Tina. Finally Tina offered to loan her a sleeveless white blouse.

Merry's mouth dropped open. "Your new one?" she asked suspiciously.

"You have to look right in case he—I mean, anybody sees you," Tina said with great dignity.

Merry put on the blouse. While she buttoned it, she watched Tina through her lashes. Then Merry perched on the edge of the lower bunk to change thongs for white anklets and sandals. "I s'pose I have to comb my hair, too," she said crossly.

"Why not?" Tina retorted.

"It's a waste of time, that's why not," Merry said. She jerked the rubber bands from the ends of her heavy dark braids. Her fingers pushed through the loops of hair to loosen her braids. A mass of dark curls bounced when she moved. Impishly Merry teased, "I think I'll just go unbraided and let the wind blow my hair."

"Merry, you wouldn't!" Tina wailed.

"Tina, what's the matter with you tonight?" Merry asked shortly. "You're hard to get along with."

"I—I just mean you have so—so much hair. I mean, it's prettier when it is braided neatly." Tina kept her back to Merry. When she looked up, she realized she was facing the mirror. Merry could see her cheeks turn red. Abruptly Tina dived for her own suitcase. She pretended to hunt for a handkerchief.

"You have a clean hankie in your blouse pocket," Merry reminded. "I see the corner sticking out."

"Oh. Oh, yes." Tina fumbled at her pocket. She rose so quickly she bumped her head on a bunk ladder. This gave her an excuse to ooze out a tear while she rubbed her head.

Tina hurried out of the trailer. She met Penny near the clothesline. "You need a clean play-suit," Tina told her smallest sister.

Penny's sensitive face crumpled. "I changed since noon," she told Tina.

"Then change again," Tina snapped. When she realized how shortly she had spoken, Tina turned to apologize. She was too late. Penny had already entered the trailer and shut the door.

No matter how hard she argued, there was nothing Tina could do about the way Terry and Tom looked. They put on clean jeans and white T-shirts. When they swished a brush through flattops, they were dressed. Tina writhed inwardly. She recalled Whitney Blake's starched shirt, sports jacket, and slacks. Terry and Tom owned clothes just as nice. She did not dare suggest they wear them to return a can of gasoline. Not even Mother would understand that request!

Grandma's Spanish rice disappeared so fast Father insisted it had not been chewed. Terry and Merry, Penny and Tom rushed to the dock to put on their safety belts, but Tina made a special trip to Grandma's bedroom. There she stood in front of the door mirror. She wondered, "Do I look all right?" She tried to see herself through the eyes of one who lived in that big house at the edge of the water. She gave up. She had never been in that house, or in any house like it. She could not judge. It was like trying to measure cloth without a tape measure. Suddenly Tina felt so confused and unsure, she almost decided not to go.

Then Terry shouted, "I thought you were in a hurry, Tina!"

Tina cast one last glance at her smoothly brushed page boy. She hurried to the dock. All the grown-up Tuckers hovered around the boat.

"Fasten your safety belts!" Mother cautioned.

"Don't stand up in the boat," Grandma

chirped as she waved them off.

"Check your gas before you start home," Father advised.

Grandpa boomed, "Have fun, maties!"

Tina tilted a tremulous smile at Grandpa. How could she tell Grandpa he had given the one bit of advice she could not follow? Who could have fun, feeling as mixed up as a potato salad?

All the way down the length of Lake Annabelle Tina instructed her brothers and sisters in proper speech and manners. "Remember to say thank you for the gas," she told Terry a half dozen times. Finally he burst out, "Do I have to roll over and bark three times, too?"

Merry giggled, but Tina did not think Terry's joke was funny. "*You* could be a little bit more dignified," she told Merry primly.

Tina turned to Penny. "If he—I mean, anybody speaks to you, be sure to answer."

Merry rushed to Penny's defense. "My goodness, Tina Tucker, we probably won't even see

Whitney Blake. His father may be on the dock."

Tina flushed. She twisted long, slim fingers. Oh, my goodness, what would she do if Merry happened to be right? She had spent the whole weekend worrying about meeting the son. It had not occurred to her that she might meet the father instead. Oh. Oh, my!

When the Tuckers came in sight of the Blake house, Tom pointed out a spot of blue alongside the boat dock. "There's that boat that costs so much," he rumbled.

"Tom!" Tina wailed. "Don't ask anybody how much that boat costs."

"Don't have to," Terry said, shrugging. "I saw a picture in a boating magazine."

"Me, too," Tom said, nodding soberly.

Helplessly Tina looked at her brothers. Boys, even very small boys like Tom, knew so many things she did not know. Why was it so hard to teach them dress and manners?

Well. It was too late to make changes. There,

across that smooth sheet of water, stood Whitney Blake.

"He doesn't see us," Tom declared. "He didn't wave."

Terry scowled. "He did, too, see us. Look at that dive!"

From the high board at the end of the dock the tall boy performed a difficult dive. He faced forward, bounded into the air, and flipped in a back somersault.

"Oh, boy," Merry said softly. "That was a nice gainer."

At once the boy returned to the dock with a clean, swift Australian crawl. His next dive was a half-gainer. Again the Blake boy jumped from a front-dive take-off position. This time his back dive was accompanied with a toe-touching jackknife. Before the heavy, slow Tub reached the Blake dock, the boy had completed a swan, a jackknife, and a back flip. Terry did not join in the chorus of "Oh" and "Ah." He growled, "That guy is showing off."

Oh, was he really? Tina wondered with a catch in her throat. Was this tall, dark boy trying to impress the Tuckers? That was not necessary. *One* Tucker was already impressed.

"Who cares?" Merry answered Terry's growl. "I want Whitney to show me how to do that swan dive without falling in a heap."

Ungallantly Terry told his twin, "You can use help. Your swan dive is a dead duck."

Merry flared back, "Yours isn't any better, Terence Tucker!"

The boy turned his head, but his glance slid past the prow of the Tub.

"Ssh," Tina warned the arguing twins. "Voices carry on water. He will hear you."

Terry was steering the Tub. He turned the throttle on the motor handle to idle. His shoulders lifted in an impatient shrug when he faced Tina. "What of it?" he asked.

Tom turned. He let his eyes travel over Tina's warm face. He announced soberly, "Tina likes that Colin Whitney Blake better than she likes us."

"Oh, I do not!" Tina insisted so loudly the boy turned his head. He looked straight at Tina as Terry allowed the Tub to wash to the dock. Whitney's eyes were dark and alert. Almost at once he shifted his glance to Terry and became very much concerned with the docking of the Tub.

Tina huddled on the middle seat beside Penny.

She stared at the toes of her sandals while Terry delivered the gasoline can. Oh. Oh, my. Even her own tongue had embarrassed her. What could she do now?

10
The Other End
of the Lake

After delivering the gasoline can to Whitney Blake, Terry lost no time in starting the Tub's motor.

Tina tried to think of some way to say good-bye to Whitney Blake without calling attention to herself. To her pleased relief, Whitney held the side of the boat. "Come up to the sun deck for ice cream?" he invited. His smile included all the Tuckers.

Tom straightened with interest. Even Terry forgot to scowl. Merry and Penny turned to face Tina. Their blue eyes asked questions.

"There are so many of us," Merry said with hesitation.

The boy chuckled. "That's all right. Dad made lots of ice cream."

At the mention of cookery, Tina's blond head jerked up. Tina wanted to be a superior cook some day. She tried to picture the dignified senator in a kitchen. She gave up when her mental picture included a ruffled apron over a long black robe. She eyed Whitney. "Your *father* made the ice cream?" she asked warily.

The Blake boy shrugged. "Sure," he told Tina. "Dad likes to cook."

Whitney steadied the boat. He held out a hand to assist Merry, Penny, and Tina. They stepped onto the canvas topped dock. There they stood in a row, elbow to elbow, while Terry and Whitney moored the old Tub beside the sleek blue boat called Lady. Then the five Tuckers followed the senator's son down the dock and through the door in the basement wall.

Coolness flowed along Tina's skin when she stepped into a dim, large room with a cement floor. Tom pushed through the group. He stood alone with hands on hips. Before Tina grasped Tom's attention, Tom walked to a wall. He touched it with his fingers. Then he sat on his heels and placed the palms of both plump hands on the floor. Tom circled the whole room, carefully examining walls and floor. When he returned to the group he asked, speaking in his deepest voice, "Is this a basement?"

"Yes," Whitney answered.

Tom shrugged. "Guess it doesn't have water in it," was all he said. But Tom kept looking back at the walls as the group climbed wide cement steps to an open sun deck.

In the area behind one of the round towers, several people in comfortable sun clothing sat in lounge chairs. They were eating pink ice cream.

Tom nodded with approval. "I like strawberry," he told the Blake boy.

Tina's eyes darted an apology to Whitney Blake, but he did not notice. He was grinning at Tom. Obviously Whitney saw nothing wrong with Tom's manners.

Whitney beckoned with one hand. He walked toward a slim, tall woman who was deep in conversation with a white-haired man. This woman must be Whitney's mother, Tina decided. Although she was strawberry blond while Whitney was dark, they shared the same alert, lean look. The minute Whitney's back was turned, Tina whispered in Tom's ear, "Ssh, wait until his mother invites you to have ice cream."

Tom nodded.

Tina forgot about Tom when she saw that she was within touching distance of a senator's wife. Tina gulped. She drew three deep breaths for self-control, just the way her piano teacher instructed before a recital. Then she found she was able to push her stiff face into a smile. Her tongue even murmured, "How do you do?" Whitney performed introductions with so much ease, Tina looked reproachfully at Merry. At her first opportunity, Tina would remind Merry to notice Whitney's manners.

A blond girl with a ponytail and bangs came from the house. She crossed the deck. She gave Whitney's mother a white sweater. Tina was lost in admiration. She could see no flaw in the girl whose hair style she had tried to copy.

"My cousin, Ruth Ann," Whitney announced. "Tina Tucker."

Ruth Ann murmured and Tina mumbled. Tina

glanced back, unable to take her eyes from the girl. Ruth Ann was even prettier than her picture. The girl sat on the arm of the chair occupied by the white-haired man. She called him Pop. She combed his hair with her fingers, just the way Penny liked to comb Grandpa's wispy white hair.

Suddenly Tina's toe bumped something. She lurched. Her eyes looked down, then up.

Oh! Oh, no! She had walked right into a very tall, broad-chested man with a sunburned face and bushy eyebrows. Something wiggled under Tina's foot. She looked down to discover the man wore thongs. Her own sandal was planted on the tip of one of his rubber soles. She had barely missed his large, bare toes. Hastily Tina moved her foot. In an agony of confusion she gasped, "S'cuse me." With another wild glance at the big man, she added, "S-Sir!" knowing this must be Senator Blake, Whitney Blake's father.

Tina put her feet so close together her ankle bones rubbed. Oh—oh! Had one of her brothers

or sisters seen her walk on the senator's foot?
And, oh, oh—oh! Had Whitney Blake seen? If
he had, she would simply die.

"Won't you have some ice cream?" invited the
senator. His red face creased in a friendly grin.

At Tina's shoulder Whitney said, "Dad, this
is Tina Tucker, a friend of mine."

"Any friend of yours is a friend of mine," the
senator said heartily. Tina heard the teasing
friendliness in the man's voice. She knew this
man was his son's best friend and was willing
to be her friend. Tina drew a trembling breath.
She accepted the big mound of pink ice cream the
senator scooped from a freezer.

Merry, Terry, and Penny accepted plates of
ice cream. They sat in the lounge chairs Whitney
offered.

But Tom stood aside. He scrubbed his flattop
with one plump hand. He stared at the flags
fluttering from the tower. He licked his lips with
his tongue. He stood close to Tina and gazed wist-

fully across the deck at Mrs. Blake.

Then Tom sauntered to Merry's chair. Hopefully he watched Mrs. Blake.

Merry scooped up a big bite. She let it melt on her tongue. She looked up at Tom. Incredulously she asked, "Don't you want ice cream, Tom?"

Terry was sitting on a wrought iron footstool beside Merry. "Yeah," he said, eying Tom with concern. "I've never seen you refuse strawberry."

Tom was hungry. Of all foods in the world, he liked strawberry ice cream best. His voice was deep as a well when he answered, "Colin Whitney Blake's mother didn't ask me."

Tina had been trying to swallow her own embarrassment with the cool, sweet dessert. "Tom!" she wailed helplessly.

Tom's face was unsmiling. "But, Tina, you said—" he reminded.

"Yes, Tina," Terry put in. "You said, 'Wait till his mother asks you.'"

Tina felt her cheeks blaze. She swept an imploring glance from the senator to his wife. Ordinarily the Tuckers were a happy, well-mannered group of children—but from their first contact with these Blakes, nothing had gone right. What must Whitney think of them?

A chuckle rippled around the group. Tina's cheeks blazed hot, then hotter. Then she realized the people were laughing with Tom and not at him.

Mrs. Blake reached out a graceful hand and pulled Tom to her side. "If that is what Tina said, that is just what you should do, Tom," she smiled approvingly. Then she asked very politely, "Will you have some ice cream, Tom Tucker? It's strawberry."

"Made by my two hands," boomed the senator.

"I picked the strawberries out of our own garden," Whitney added in the same amused, coaxing tone used by his parents.

Tom did not have to be coaxed. "Yes, please,"

he answered with huge relief.

When all the plates were emptied, the senator insisted on doling out seconds. With a solemn wink and a nod of his head, he gave the biggest mound to Tom. Ruth Ann circled the deck with a tray of cookies. With surprise Tina noticed they were honey wafers instead of the good homemade cookies Grandma would have served.

Merry and Ruth Ann burst out laughing when they met for the first time since the recital. They carried their ice cream to a small table apart from the group. Suddenly Penny said, a little shakily, "It's getting dark."

With surprise Tina saw daylight was going. A dim coolness spread across the woods. The smooth, green lawn which sloped up behind the large house was dotted with robins.

"We'd better go home," Tom announced soberly. "Grandpa's boat doesn't move very fast."

With a catch of anxious excitement in her throat, Tina realized that Penny and Tom were right. It would be nearly dark by the time the heavy old Tub reached home.

"Maybe you'd better take the children home, Whit," Mrs. Blake suggested.

Tina had been surprised to learn the dignified senator made ice cream. Now she was startled to hear him called by a shortened name.

Quickly Terry said, "Oh, we'll make it," just as if he traveled alone in a boat every night.

Tina saw Mrs. Blake raise nicely arched eyebrows, then glance at her husband.

Tina explained, "Father is turning on the dock light to be sure we find our way home. This is the first time we have ever gone out of our bay alone after supper."

Mrs. Blake's relief was plain to see. She urged the senator, "I think you should go with the children to be sure they reach home safely, Whit."

Terry glowered. He muttered to Tina, "Did you have to say that?" Tina saw his cheeks turn

red. His ears began to glow. Tina knew Terry
was in a "slow burn." When Terry used Grandpa's putt-putting fishing motor, he pretended his
speed was fifty miles per hour. With the long,
blue Lady alongside, idling faster than the Tub's
top speed, Terry could not pretend. Tina was
sorry Terry would feel robbed of the adventure
of night-boating.

"Would you like a spin around the lake,
Madge?" the senator asked his wife.

Madge Blake turned to invite her guests to
share the boat ride. When they agreed, she rose.
"I'd love it, Whit," she announced. "I seldom see
the other end of the lake."

"It isn't the other end of the world," Terry
muttered in Merry's ear.

Tina overheard. She glanced quickly to see if
one of the Blakes or their guests had heard her
brother's rude comment. Evidently they had not,
for they were gathering up lightweight sweaters.
Ruth Ann and Whitney collected plates and

spoons. Then Whitney joined the Tuckers. "Mind
if I ride with you?" he asked. "Dad has a boat-
load."

"Come on," Tom invited. "We have lots of
room." Tom swaggered because he could play
host to a Blake, but Terry dragged his feet.

Halfway down the stairs, Tom stopped to
look around. "Are you sure this is your basement?" he asked Whitney.

Whitney grinned. "I'm sure," he said.

"Well, it's a good one," Tom decided. "It's
dry."

"Thank you," Whitney said gravely, but his
eyes danced.

When the Tuckers reached the Tub, the senator supervised the seating. Merry whispered to
Tina, "He's making a noise like a father."

"Ssh," Tina warned, but she looked at the
man with new understanding. A few hours ago
he had been a person to fear, because he was
unknown and a senator. Suddenly he fitted into

a familiar pattern. He was a father.

And Mrs. Blake was a mother, interested in the safety of children. Had she really meant to sound as snobbish as Terry thought? Across zigzagging evening shadows, Tina watched the senator's wife in the blue boat. Mrs. Blake pointed out the beaches, the shadowed coves and the jutting rocks. Guests watched and exclaimed. Tina wondered when they crossed the invisible line to the "other end" of Lake Annabelle.

Tina loved every lapping wave and every inch of shoreline. She did not want a line drawn down the middle of the lake. She did not want to separate the Tuckers and their neighbors in cottages from the large summer residences on the bay where the senator lived.

Since Tom had made the clipping book, Tina had spun like a phonograph record. She knew that some people had power, others had not; some people had money, others had very little; and some lived in large houses, while others

did not. She knew the Tuckers were some place
in the middle, between the haves and have-nots.
But she had a very confused idea of how all those
other people lived.

Tina loved her family. Suddenly it became
very important to her that all those other people
think well of the Tuckers. Whitney Blake was
one of those "other people."

11

Tina In Charge

Terry did not enjoy the return from the Blake house to Grandpa's cottage. He had planned to roar down the lake like a returning hero. Instead, the Lady idled not twenty feet from the Tub's starboard side and threw out big waves for Terry to plow. While the Tub putt-putted at top speed, the Lady, loaded with Blakes and their neighbors, purred with harnessed power. Terry felt like a milkman trying to force his milk-wagon plug to pace a race horse. This irked Terry. He loved the old Tub.

Having Whitney Blake for a passenger did not improve Terry's temper. Whitney took up too much of Merry's attention to suit Terry. Even

182

Penny talked easily and forgot to be shy. Tom asked endless questions about the senator's basement. Only Tina was silent.

For a while Terry tried to talk to Tina. When she did not answer, Terry hunched his shoulders and turned his back on the rest of the children. When he stared down the bridge of his own short nose, he did not see the blue Lady. "I can find my way home without help!" he muttered under his breath.

Soon Terry found it was not easy to locate the landmarks which were so familiar in daylight. Dusky light seemed to wrap woods, water, and sky in a gray scarf. It was not dark enough to identify summer homes by the arrangement of lighted windows. He knew the squares of light behind the woods glowed in farmhouses, but they looked so much alike Terry became confused. Pretending confidence he did not feel, Terry picked out lights beyond the woods which separated lake and farmland and turned the boat toward a flickering shore-light.

Merry bumped one of Terry's shins with a foot. "We aren't home yet!" she said sharply.

Terry jabbed a finger at the lighted spot in the woods. "That's the Cooper farm," he argued. "It's up above our sandbar, so that has to be our dock light."

Silently the Tuckers studied the shore. Out of the dusk came Tom's husky voice. "The Cooper farm is south of our sandbar. You said so."

"Well, that's south!" Terry snapped.

Merry snapped right back, "That isn't our dock light. The light is on the wrong side of that blackness." The blackness Merry mentioned was the part of the shoreline Terry thought was the sandbar at the mouth of the brook.

"Where is south?" Tom asked Whitney.

The Blake boy had kept silent during the argument. Terry was so sure Whitney could not answer, he almost liked the boy. Instead, Whitney tilted his chin up toward the stars breaking through the grayness. "There's the Big Dipper, and there's the Little Dipper, see?" he asked.

Terry retorted, "So what?" but he looked at the sky.

"The North Star is the tip of the handle of the Little Dipper," Whitney explained.

"Huh," Terry grunted.

"Grandpa used to be a sailor," Tom told Whitney. "He knows about stars, too."

A big wave rocked the Tub as the Lady pulled alongside. "Having trouble, skipper?" the senator boomed.

"Not now," Terry answered briefly. Although he was forced to accept the Blake boy's facts, Terry refused to look at Colin Whitney Blake. He swerved back onto the course he had laid out for himself before it grew so dark. The rest of the way home, Terry kept his eyes on the blue Lady and allowed the senator to take the lead.

Terry was glad when the shape of the land and the position of the lights lined up in a known

pattern. Above the lake were the Cooper farm
lights. Below and to the left was Green Fields,
where Anne Green lived. Grandpa's cottage was
last in the row of lights near the beach. And
there was the dock light, with the tall cottonwoods on the beach for a black background.

"Father is waiting for us," Penny said happily.

Father hallooed across the black water, and
the children answered. An echo repeated and
jumbled voices. Carefully Terry steered the Tub
to its usual mooring space, more relieved to be
home than he liked to admit. Water rolled over
the end of the dock when the long blue Lady
pulled opposite the Tub. Father moved quickly
to protect his shoes, then he held out his hand lest
one Tucker miss the edge of the dock and step
into water. Like a sea captain, Terry was last to
leave the Tub.

Tina walked to the middle of Grandpa's dock.
She made introductions, carefully and distinctly.

A murmur of "How do you do?" came out of the long blue boat. The senator reached over the steering wheel to shake hands with Father.

Sleepily Penny started down the dock toward shore. She turned to tell Father, "They gave us strawberry ice cream."

"Colin Whitney Blake's father made it," Tom added throatily.

Cheerfully Father asked, "Did you save some ice cream for me?"

"Oh, Father!" Tina whispered fiercely, but the senator covered her words with a chuckle.

"Come down any time, Tucker," the senator invited. "I'll let you sample my ice cream."

Father's cordial manner matched that of the senator. "When you're at our end of the lake, drop in, Senator. The women around here keep the coffee pot on. Tina makes the cookies."

The Blake boy was seating himself beside his cousin, Ruth Ann. When Father mentioned Tina's cookies, he turned his head. In the light cast by the dock light, Tina forgave Father for his undignified question.

The senator touched the starter and the motor began to purr. "Thanks for the boat ride," Whitney called.

Terry did not answer, but Merry sang out, "Welcome." She started down the dock, then turned to shout, "Come to lunch tomorrow, Whitney."

Flinging up spray, the blue and white boat roared away from the dock and down the center of the lake.

Anxiously Tina asked Merry, "Did he say yes?"

Merry shrugged and patted a yawn. "I'm not sure," she admitted. "Let's wait till tomorrow and see if he shows up."

"Merry!" Tina gasped. "We can't treat a senator's son like—like Jim Jackson!"

"Why not?" Merry asked impatiently. "Let's go to bed. Looking at all those stars made me

sleepy. I can hardly keep my eyes open."

Merry and Penny went to sleep the minute the lights were turned off in the trailer. Tina lay awake for a long time. She thought about the Blake boy's unexpected invitation to join his family on the sun deck. She must remember to tell Mother about the flags on the towers.

When Tina awoke the next morning, birds were feeding noisily and cheerily. In the lower bunk opposite her own, Mother still slept. With her blond hair tumbled on the pillow, Mother looked young. Her lips curled up at the corners as if she dreamed of pleasant things.

Merry's feet were uncovered and her blanket was a bright red tangle. One of Penny's fragile-looking hands hung over the edge of her mattress. Tina touched Penny's palm, ever so gently, and Penny's fingers curled.

Tina smiled. She loved wake-up time.

Suddenly Tina sat up straight in bed. This was tomorrow, and Whitney Blake was invited to lunch! She scrambled out of bed, pulling her pajama top over her head as she rose.

Sleepily Penny pushed back her hair and peered down at Tina. "Whatcha doin', Tina?" she murmured.

"Getting up," Tina answered briskly. "We have work to do. Wake Merry."

Penny spoke two or three times, then threw her pillow. It landed on Merry's stomach. Merry batted the pillow aside and muttered, "Who threw that?"

"I did," Penny chirped. "You're supposed to wake up."

"Who says so?" Merry mumbled and prepared to go back to sleep.

By this time Tina was dressed in shorts, T-shirt, and sandals. She tickled the sole of one of Merry's bare feet. "Get up, Merry," Tina urged. "Company is coming."

Merry groaned. "Ohhh. Not till lunch—and who cares, anyway?"

"I do," Tina said, so softly she was not heard. She left the trailer and stepped into the backyard. Dew still clung to the tufts of grass which managed to live in the much-used area. Juncos scratched like tiny, black-capped chickens. A fat robin listened for worms in the hard-beaten path, ran a few steps and listened again.

Toby had slept in a nest of dry grass under the trailer. He crawled out, stretched, and flopped his big ears till they snapped. He walked beside Tina, leaning heavily. Her fingertips dug into the curly fur around his collar.

When Tina opened the kitchen screen door, Grandpa turned from a mirror on the wall. He was shaving, and lather covered his face. He kissed the air and waggled his fingers at Tina. Then he returned to the exacting task of shaving. Grandpa had nothing to say before morning coffee.

Knowing this, Tina crossed the room and drew water into the coffeepot. While she measured

out the fragrant coffee, her eyes moved down
the shoreline of Lake Annabelle. Morning smoke
was a gray haze in the sky to show where York-
ville lay. And, someplace in that blue distance,
flags waved on the round towers of the Blake
house.

It was hard for Tina to believe she had actually
eaten strawberry ice cream in a senator's house.

And now a senator's son was invited to lunch.
It was like entertaining royalty.

While Grandpa's coffee bubbled, Tina opened
the refrigerator, the cooler, and the cupboards.
She was discouraged by what she saw. The ham
was pared down to the bone. Several wings and
backs of chicken had been fried Sunday. The cake
which had been a chocolate joy was dry and hard.
Probably Terry had left the cover off the cake
box.

Grandpa splashed cold water on his pink
cheeks. "Hunting for something, matie?" he
asked heartily.

Unhappily Tina told him, "There isn't a thing to eat."

Grandpa looked surprised. After all, Grandma was one of Yorkville's best cooks. Drily he told Tina, "I don't think you'll starve."

"Oh, I'm not hungry," Tina said quickly.

Grandpa said, "Humph," and set about combing his wispy white hair.

Up on the sleeping porch, feet thumped the floor. Tina knew Father was getting up. Grandma sang in the bedroom, while she made her bed. Sugar crossed the cool kitchen linoleum. He jumped onto a windowsill to stare at a robin.

Tina wanted to sing, just because loved people were doing familiar things. But Whitney was invited to lunch. The song drained down her throat. Tina gulped and squinted through her eyelashes. She tried to pick out the distant shores where Whitney lived. What was he going to wear today? What did he like to eat? What would he talk about? What—?

"Coffee perked yet?" Grandpa grunted.

Tina brought a cup from the cupboard. She poured Grandpa's coffee and watched him taste. "Don't burn your tongue, Grandpa," she cautioned.

"Humph," was his answer, but smile crinkles began to deepen at the corners of his eyes and mouth. By the time his cup was empty, his usual happy morning-rumble of words filled the kitchen. "Good coffee, matie," he said heartily.

Tina smiled. *I love you, Grandpa*, she thought. She did not say the words aloud. It was not necessary. Grandpa understood.

If only it were as easy to understand other people, and to be understood by them.

Grandpa winked and carried his coffee to the yard for a morning look at Lake Annabelle. Tina carried nine plates from the cupboard. She circled the big kitchen table to put them in place for breakfast. While she laid the stainless steel flatware, Tina recalled the series of embarrassments she had suffered since the morning she had asked Tom to clip those pictures. She muttered to herself, "Whitney Blake must think we are a family of clowns."

The more closely Tina looked at the Tuckers through Blake eyes, the hotter she felt. "I'll show him!" Tina determined, clenching her teeth.

Tom came down the stairs, carrying his shoes.

"Put your shoes on, and go pick up all the toys in the yard," she said crisply.

"Before breakfast?" he asked, deep in his throat. He stood on one foot like a heron and considered Tina's order.

"Yes," she said briskly. "I'll find something else for you to do after breakfast."

And she did. The minute breakfast was over, Tina began to give orders. "Terry, you can take all the caps and jackets and fishing tackle off the kitchen wall. Merry, pick up all the magazines and books and put them where they belong. Penny, gather up all your paper dolls. Tom—"

"I put away my toys," Tom interrupted.

"I know." Tina's blue eyes flashed. "Now you can rake the yard."

Tina's brothers and sisters lined up at the kitchen door. Merry was spokesman. "Why are we doing all this work?" she demanded. "I'd rather pitch horseshoes with Terry. We didn't finish our game last night. He is a ringer and a leaner ahead of me!"

"I have a pink paper-doll dress to finish," Penny ventured timidly.

"Toby has some burrs in his fur," Tom declared. "He wants me to comb them out."

All four of the younger Tuckers had made plans, but Tina considered her own plan more important. She was going to prove to a Blake that the Tuckers were nice people to know and visit.

"Company!" Tina reminded. She dumped soap in a mop pail and prepared to mop the large kitchen floor. The rest of the Tuckers moved at snail-pace. They carried out Tina's orders, but they grumbled.

Before Mother and Grandma knew what was going on, beds were made and clothing was put away. Tina was dusting the living room when Mother entered. She carried a litter of curlers, bobby pins, and hair spray. She wore faded bermudas and an old white blouse. Without use of a mirror, Mother began to roll her wet blond hair.

"Mother!" Tina wailed. "You aren't going to pin your hair this morning!"

"I always pin my hair in the morning," said Mother calmly. "Do you want me to be in curlers when your father comes home?"

Close to tears, Tina burst out, "But we've invited company!"

Mother paused with a curl half rolled. "Nobody told me," she said. She looked around the orderly room. "Who are we entertaining? A dignitary?"

Tina was as dramatic as Merry when she explained, *"Mother*, we are entertaining *Whitney Blake!"*

With a sigh of relief Mother rolled another curl. "Oh. If it's just a boy who's expected—"

"Just a boy!" Tina repeated, raising her voice. "Mother, you didn't *hear* me. *Whitney*—"

"I heard you," Mother interrupted calmly.

12
"Make up Time!"

By noon the Tucker household was totally upset. "And it's all your fault!" Merry told Tina.
Merry scowled her fiercest and drummed the
kitchen floor with her heels. "This is the wrong-
est day I've ever had!"

"Don't mark the floor," Tina said sharply.

"What else is there to do?" Tom asked huskily.
"You won't let us play."

Tom, Penny, Merry, and Terry sat in chairs
lined up along the kitchen wall. They wore the
playsuits reserved for Sunday afternoons. Merry's braids were so tight her eyebrows lifted.
Terry bunched toes in his best shoes and grumbled, "My feet are hot."

201

"You can stand shoes for a few minutes more," Tina said coolly. "It's almost noon."

Grandma bustled into the kitchen, tying the bows of a stiff white apron. She peeked in Grandpa's shaving mirror, patted her white hair, then trotted to the stove. Cautiously, she opened the oven door. When Grandma straightened, she faced Tina and said severely, "If that boy doesn't come soon, my cheese souffle will be completely ruined."

"He'll be here soon, Grandma," Tina said hastily. It was always upsetting to hear Grandma scold.

"You will remember I suggested toasted cheese sandwiches," Grandma reminded her. "They can be made ahead of the hour and toasted as needed."

"But your souffle is so good and pretty," Tina cried, hearing the quaver in her own voice.

"Souffle is neither good nor pretty when it falls," Grandma snapped. She trotted from the kitchen to the living room. Her white apron bow bobbed with every step she took.

Mother came from the backyard with a handful of wildflowers. A few white petals dropped on the linoleum. Tina ran for the dustpan and swept them up. Mother shrugged. She did not smile when she told Tina, "These won't make a good table centerpiece. The petals will fall in our food before we finish lunch."

"I wanted them because they are pretty," Tina

explained. Helplessly she stopped in the middle of a sentence. From wake-up hour till noon Tina had been driving the whole family. She had driven herself hardest of all. So tired and nervous she could cry over nothing, Tina stood in the middle of the kitchen and twisted her hands. She had spoiled the morning, and she knew it. But what could she do? Whitney Blake was invited to lunch, and he was a senator's son.

Timidly Penny suggested, "We could eat lunch out on the picnic table. The lake is pretty to look at."

"The *picnic* table!" Tina cried. "Penny, you saw the Blakes' sun deck. They don't eat on the beach."

"That's 'cause they don't have a beach," Tom said wisely. "They have a basement under the water." Tom considered that unusual room at the end of the dock. "But it's dry," he finished soberly.

"Who cares?" Terry grumbled. "I'm hungry,

and I want to go swimming. If that guy doesn't come pretty soon, we won't be able to swim before dark."

All eyes turned toward the clock above the range. They were not allowed to swim for an hour after any meal. The later the meal, the later the swim.

Grandma bustled to a window. "Are you sure that boy is coming here today?" she asked impatiently.

"No," Tina admitted unhappily, "but Merry asked him."

"Then why all this fuss?" Grandma asked sharply.

This time all eyes turned toward Tina. "He— he—" Tina stammered. "We—we—" How could she explain her confusion? She had never known a senator's son until she met Whitney Blake. In her imagination she had placed the Blake family on a hill so high she could only stand at the bottom and look up.

Each time a Tucker had met a Blake, Tina's pride had suffered. She could not be happy until she regained her pride in being a Tucker. She had worked hard all day to erase the bad impression the Tuckers had made on the Blakes. She was not going to give up just because lunch was late.

Because she was hungry, unhappy, and confused, nothing looked right to Tina. The kitchen was stripped of all signs of camp living. She had coaxed Grandma to put a tablecloth over the oilcloth. The dishes off the highest shelf, and the silver out of the chest had been laid with care. But they just did not look right in a cottage kitchen.

Tina turned to the window to hide the tears which threatened. For the first time in her life she noticed the ragged grass in the yard. She pictured the lawn behind the Blake house, a slope of green velvet. There, dozens of orange-breasted robins walked about in the last small patches of sunlight when evening fell.

Down at Grandpa's boat dock the heavy old Tub looked clumsy and weatherbeaten when Tina thought of the sleek blue Lady.

Here at Grandpa's cottage there was no sun deck furnished with a dozen wrought iron chairs and settees piled with bright corduroy cushions. Here, a long narrow yard overlooked beach and bay. A hammock between two trees sagged from use. Grandma's faded chaise lounge was beside Grandpa's old brown leather chair. A few slatted wooden chairs sat around the yard. When more seating space was needed, Grandpa brought wooden benches from a lean-to shed beside the garage.

Tina loved every spear of grass, every grain of sand, every worn piece of furniture—but when she tried to look through Blake eyes, everything changed. Tina saw the shabbiness and overlooked the comfort.

What was she to do? Grandma was upset.

Mother had turned silent. Her brothers and sisters were hot and unhappy. Even Toby lay under the table with his head on his front paws. Once in the while he peeked out. When no happy voices or waggling figures invited Toby to play, he lay down again. Only Sugar was happy. The cat liked quiet.

Minutes dragged. Grandma trotted to the oven again. She clicked her tongue and frowned. Mother propped up the drooping flowers. Penny wiggled in her chair, then smoothed the wrinkles from her starched playsuit. Terry cracked his knuckles while Tom stared at a picture on a calendar. Merry folded her hands across her chest and scowled at Tina.

At twelve thirty Tina walked to a window and propped her elbows on the sill. She stared down the lake. No boat was in sight.

A heavy silence settled in the room that usually rang with happy voices. Tina wanted to return to normal, but she did not know how. If only Mother or Grandma would give an order, she would obey gladly. Hopefully she turned her head, but neither said a word. They waited.

"Kiss and make up" was a rule in the Tucker house, carried out in a gay ceremony which took the sting out of being at fault. Tina wanted to cry out, "Make up time!" and break the silence, but she did not feel like kissing anybody, even Penny. Tears began to roll down Tina's cheeks. She turned to look at her brothers and sisters, sitting in an unhappy, silent row. Oh, what was she doing to all the people she loved most? She wanted to make up with them. "Let's—" Tina began.

Somebody stepped onto the back porch. Hastily Tina scrubbed her eyes and blew her nose with her hankie.

Tom slid off his chair. He announced, "Here's Colin Whitney Blake. Now we can eat."

Whitney peered through the screen door at the silent, sober Tuckers. "I'm sorry I'm late," he said. "I didn't know what time to come. It took longer than I expected on my motor bike."

Merry pushed open the screen door. "For goodness' sake, Whitney, come in," she said impatiently. "We're starved."

There was an awkward scramble for chairs. Tina had instructed Terry to pull out Mother's chair, but he forgot. He scowled when Whitney seated Mother. Whitney noticed the scowl and threw a startled glance around the room to see what he had done wrong. Penny tipped over her milk glass and looked stricken. Mother ran for a mop-up cloth. Merry reached for a stalk of celery and crunched noisily.

Usually Grandma beamed with pride when she carried food to the table. Today she plopped a soggy souffle on a pad in front of Mother. "It fell," she announced crisply.

Tina blinked. She swallowed hard, but a tear rolled down her cheek. She was aware of Whitney's watchful brown eyes, but now it no longer mattered. The day was ruined.

Silently the Tuckers ate, then mumbled, "S'cuse me," and escaped to the yard. There they sat and stared at the lake, waiting for an hour to pass. Tina sat on the edge of a wooden chair. She stared across the yard at Whitney Blake who also sat on the edge of his chair. Suddenly she wished she had never seen the picture in the paper. The Blakes had brought nothing but trouble in her life.

Jumping to her feet, Tina said loudly, "Make up time!" She rushed across the yard, grabbed Tom and squeezed him tightly. Tom hugged Penny and Penny kissed Merry. Merry rubbed noses with Terry. Terry clasped both Tina's hands and swung her in a gay dance. This was the Tucker's own special way to make up. The five joined hands and bounced in a circle. At last they fell on the ground, panting and giggling. Terry clapped Tina on the shoulder and yelled, "You're It for tree tag!" Merry, Penny, Tom, and Terry dived to touch trees.

Tom yelled at Whitney, "Touch a tree before Tina catches you!"

The warning came too late. Tina tagged Whitney and sprinted for the young cedar in the corner of the yard. Whitney saw Terry edge away from the white-barked birch and zigzag toward Tina's cedar. Two could not use the same tree, so Tina ran for the lilac tree.

For several minutes the Tuckers and Whitney Blake darted and whirled, tagged and sprinted. When they were out of breath, they ran around the side of the house to snatch beach towels from the clothesline. They threw the towels to the ground and collapsed with sprawling arms and legs.

To Tina's surprise she discovered Whitney flat on his back with his arms flung wide like the wings of a kite. He was as crumpled and dust-smeared as Terry. "*This* is what I thought it would be like at your house," Whitney said.

Tom rolled over on his stomach. He propped his face in his hands and stared into Whitney's face with sober happiness. "You said that when we jumped in the dirt," he said.

Merry wrinkled her nose in an impish grin. "That means you've been thinking about us," she teased.

Tina waited for Whitney's answer. When it came, it was a surprise.

"Why not?" Whitney retorted. "You have fun."

"Don't you have fun?" Merry widened her dark blue eyes till the lashes pointed upward. "Willikers! Nobody around here can dive as well as you do. Isn't it fun to be best?"

Whitney shrugged. "Not when there's nobody to swim with me."

Tina thought of the girl whose hair style she had tried to copy. She asked, "Doesn't your cousin swim with you?"

"Ruth Ann?" Whitney scoffed. "She might

get wet! If she got one teeny, weeny curl out of place, the sky would fall."

Remembering the envy she had felt, Tina flushed. It had not occurred to her that perfection had its price. Loyal to the image she had built in her mind, she was forced to remind Whitney, "Ruth Ann plays the violin."

Merry chattered, "And she's better than I am. Her vibrato is good. Mr. Jones let her sit next to the audience."

Again Whitney shrugged. "Her father makes her practice. She just combs her hair and changes clothes." Whitney rolled over, dismissing Ruth Ann as a topic of conversation. "What shall we do now?" he asked eagerly.

"Do you want to see my clipping book?" Tom asked hopefully.

"Tom!" Tina cried. "Whitney doesn't want to see your scrapbook." Her face felt so hot, she did not dare look at Whitney. Oh! Things had started to go nicely. And now Tom was going to embarrass her! How could she explain those clippings?

"I can spell Blake," Tom said. Tina made shushing motions, but Tom ignored them.

To Tina's great relief Whitney turned his attention to Merry, who picked up a feather, tossed it into the air, and blew. When the feather drifted near Whitney's face, he blew it toward Terry.

"Let's see how long we can keep it in the air!"

Merry squealed and hopped on one foot.

"Tom and Penny won't have a chance," Terry objected. "They're too short."

"We'll lie on our stomachs in a circle," Tina planned.

Instantly the Tuckers and Whitney formed a circle, facing inward. Terry picked the feather out of the air. "Ready!" he tossed and blew. It took a great deal of energy to keep the feather floating. The game ended when Toby jumped over Tom's head and snapped the fluffy gray feather between his great jaws.

"Aw, nuts," Terry grumbled. "Wet feathers don't fly."

"Who cares?" Merry retorted. "It's swim time. Did you bring your swimming suit, Whitney?"

"Certainly!" Whitney told her. "It's in a saddlebag on my motor bike. I'll go get it."

"What time is it, Mother?" Merry shrieked.

"Your hour is up," Mother answered from the

kitchen where she was working.

Gladly Tina led the bathing-suit race to the trailer before Tom could bring out that clipping book to show Colin Whitney Blake.

13
No Time for Terry

From the day he came to lunch, Whitney Blake spent much time with the Tuckers. Tom was his shadow.

Terry was *not*. He avoided contact with Whitney and scowled each time Merry giggled. It seemed to Terry that Merry giggled more than usual when Whitney was around.

Today, Terry drew his heavy, curly brows together and watched Whitney take Merry's water-safety belt, beach towel, and suntan lotion from her arms. The group started down the beach path. Merry flashed her brightest smile and said, "Thank you, Whit."

Penny and Tina, Tom and Terry followed

Whitney and Merry. Out of the side of his mouth Terry grumbled, "Merry could carry her own stuff. She's got arms."

"That's manners," Tom said wisely.

"Huh, I've got manners, too," Terry retorted crossly. "But who wants to use 'em at the lake?"

Blissfully Penny said, "Whitney calls me Miss Tucker." She skipped and her beach towel caught on a branch of a bush.

Quickly Tom loosened the towel from the bush. Then he added Penny's beach things to the load in his short, plump arms. "Oh," Penny said happily, "you're nice, Tom."

"Manners," Tom told Terry. He struggled with the armload of towels and fat, kapok-filled life jackets, but he swaggered.

"Nuts," Terry grumbled. He fell behind the group, suddenly conscious of his own empty hands. His life belt was in the boat and he would rather drip-dry than carry a towel. He saw Whitney pile Merry's supplies on the dock, then turn to meet Tina and take her clutter of beach things.

Almost at once Merry and Tina pulled on bathing caps and demanded a lesson in diving. "Come on, Terry!" Merry urged. "Whitney will teach you the gainer."

Terry pretended to be very busy strapping Penny's safety belt. He did not answer. While Tina and Merry worked on swans and jack-knives, Terry lay on the dock with his face in his folded arms. Terry felt like two people wrapped in one skin. He knew he was being difficult. He did not know how to join the fun and save face at the same time. He was not ready to share Merry's time and attention with another boy. But, since Merry had played in the all-school recital, Terry had had no choice. Whitney had been part of one of the most exciting experiences of Merry's life, while Terry had not.

It even bothered Terry that Tina set the whole Blake family on a pedestal.

Terry was irked because Tom had deserted him for the boy who was one month older than Tina. It seemed to Terry that Whitney had walked into the Tucker family to take Terry's own place. Terry boiled with jealousy. He rolled his face on one hot arm and squinted up to see what was going on. Merry performed a swan dive so perfect Terry almost shouted to tell her so. He started to say, "That's a beaut!" He choked back his compliment when Whitney knelt

by the edge of the dock to help Merry bounce onto
the dock without climbing the dock ladder.

"Oh, I could dive forever!" Merry crowed.

Tina glanced toward the shallow water where
Tom and Penny paddled. "Let's put on our safety
belts and play keep-away," she suggested. "Tom
and Penny may be captains."

"I choose Colin Whitney Blake," Tom said at
once.

Penny hesitated, then chose Terry. Terry saw
her look of disappointment. He knew she had
wanted to choose Whitney.

"I don't wanta play," Terry mumbled and
escaped the beach to dress.

Grumpily Terry tramped to the Smith farm
to visit his old friends, Butch and Mel. The farm
boys had shared many hours of fun and adventure in the past. With them Terry was sure he
could drop his cranky nervousness and be himself. At the edge of the meadow he whistled their
secret signal and received no response. He cut

through the meadow and made his way to the barn to see if the boys were doing chores. There he found Mr. Smith cleaning stalls.

"Butch and Mel?" Mr. Smith repeated, after waving a rake at Terry. "They're visiting their grandparents in Chicago."

"All summer?" Terry asked wistfully.

"Oh, no," Mr. Smith answered. "We expect them back any day. Want to go up to the house for a glass of milk?"

Terry muttered, "No, thank you," and left the barn. Butch's old brown horse was in the barn-yard. Terry rubbed his nose and patted his shoulder. Then he crossed the meadow again. It seemed hotter and wider than he remembered.

When Terry reached the coolness of Grandpa's private road, Merry whizzed around the only curve. She was riding Whitney's motor bike. "It's *fun*, Terry!" she shrieked. "I'll give you a ride to the parking lot, then Whitney can teach you to ride."

Terry was tempted, but he resisted. "Nope," he muttered. He shoved both hands in his pockets and thumped down the road to the parking lot. He came in sight of Whitney, Tina, Tom, and Penny gathered in a laughing circle around Merry on the motor bike. The minute he did it, Terry wished he could join the group, but he could think of no way to explain his action. Unhappily he dodged trees and bushes till he came to the beach path. All alone, he tramped to the spring. He was glad when one of the Cooper cows poked her head through a green clump. It gave him an excuse to brandish a stick and yell.

When he dashed toward the cow, Terry discovered at least a half dozen animals ambling down a winding path. The cow called Old Owly refused to turn. She put down her head and rocked her horns.

Terry hesitated, not quite sure he should challenge Old Owly. To his great relief, she climbed a slope. The rest of the cows followed.

When Terry returned to the yard, he bragged, "The cows were in the woods. I chased them back."

"That's good," Merry said without interest. She turned eagerly to listen to Whitney.

As the days passed, Terry felt increasingly disturbed. With five in the Tucker family there had always been somebody to share a game, a hike, a swim, or a rest on a beach towel on the sand. All this had changed when Whitney Blake appeared. Terry turned from one brother or sister to another. Too often they were caught up in some activity which included Whitney. No one had time for Terry, who could be especially obnoxious when he was cranky. Tina and Merry worked on their diving lessons. During rest periods Merry and Whitney carried their violins to the next-door cottage where a neighbor owned a piano. Tina played accompaniments and flushed with pleasure every time Whitney looked at her. Merry was careful with her color choices and always kept her hair combed. Penny followed Whitney like an affectionate puppy. She glowed when he called her Miss Tucker.

Terry made a special effort to win Tom, but Tom refused to join Terry in his solitary hikes over familiar paths. "You don't laugh," Tom accused soberly. "I like to walk with Colin Whitney Blake."

"What's so funny about old Whit?" Terry retorted grumpily.

"He isn't funny. He's fun," Tom explained. Tom had a scientific turn of mind and liked to sort out truths. Soberly Tom studied Terry's face. Then he said, "Come on down to the cottonwoods. Tina is going to read her new book." Without a backward glance, Tom headed for the picnic table under the cottonwoods. Tom could not read, but he was hungry for the sound of words.

Terry hesitated. He, too, liked a read-aloud story. Almost against his will, Terry followed

Tom. He told himself he could listen without sitting next to Whitney Blake, but when he neared the cottonwoods Terry saw that Whitney had opened Tina's book. Whitney was waiting for an audience.

"*Hurry*, Terry!" Merry shrieked. "*Whitney* is going to *read* to us."

"So what?" Terry yelled back. He picked up a red and yellow beach ball and bounced it as he walked toward the group. Facing away from Whitney, Terry lay on his back on the sand. Balancing on his shoulders, Terry stuck his legs in the air and rolled the big beach ball with his bare feet. Once in the while Terry lost balance and thumped to the ground, disturbing both reader and listeners.

Finally Merry turned on Terry with a fierce scowl. "Ssh!" she ordered. "We're trying to listen to Whitney."

"Who wants to listen?" Terry grumbled. "Let's go fishing."

Hopefully Terry waited for response. All the Tuckers liked to fish. Today not even Tom paid the slightest attention to Terry's suggestion. With quick temper Terry kicked the ball so hard it bounced against a cottonwood and landed on the beach table, barely missing Whitney's dark head.

The older boy's eyes flashed. Red ran up Whitney's cheekbones, but his voice remained well controlled as he turned a page. Whitney continued reading. Merry, Tina, Penny, and Tom propped their chins in their hands and listened with close attention. Even Toby lay flat with his big head resting on his front paws. Toby's beady eyes peered from under a mass of curls.

Long before Tom was ready to stop listening, Whitney closed the book. All the Tuckers followed him to the parking lot where his motor bike stood in the shade of a maple. Terry followed, determined to organize a fishing party the minute Whitney got on that motor bike.

"Come back tomorrow!" Tina and Merry invited. "Stay all day!" Tom added.

Whitney sounded very grown-up when he told Penny, "Good-bye, Miss Tucker. May I see you tomorrow?"

Penny said nothing, but she smiled prettily when she fluttered her hand at Whitney.

The Blake boy straddled his motor bike and started home. Almost at once he shot back down the lane. Briskly he said, "I saw a herd of cattle headed toward Mrs. Green's property."

Tina gasped. "Anne Green doesn't like cows. They bother her!"

Tom did not hesitate. He trotted across the backyard and headed for the shortcut through the woods. "Let's chase them," he rumbled, deep in his throat.

Tina, Whitney, and Terry ran at Tom's heels, then Terry sprinted ahead. As he passed Tina, Terry growled, "Why didn't old Whit chase those cows? Betcha he's scared."

Tina looked outraged, but Whitney was too close for her to answer.

From the yard Merry and Penny called, "Wait for us."

The cattle had been out of the Cooper pasture long enough to scatter. It took the rest of the afternoon to round them up and return them to the meadow above lake and woods. Several times Terry found himself working with Whitney. The Blake boy followed Terry's shouts quickly and competently. Terry almost liked Whitney until they finished the job and returned to Grandpa's cottage.

Mother and Grandma were out of doors playing bridge with a couple of neighbors. When the children ran into the yard, Mother was dummy. She waved, then walked across the uneven grass. "My word, Terry, you could use a shower," she said, lifting an eyebrow.

Terry followed her glance and saw that Whitney had stayed fairly clean. Terry scowled and

pushed his dirty hands in his pockets. "Nuts!" he muttered as he stalked toward the house to obey Mother. All of the jealousy and aggravation of the summer filled Terry's throat like a bite of food too hot to swallow. He poked out his lower lip and squinted his eyes in his blackest scowl. "Tomorrow," he muttered, "we're gonna go fishin'!"

The next morning Terry woke up with one thought in mind: He was going fishing, and the rest of the Tuckers were going with him! He would show Whitney Blake who was leader.

Terry tramped down the stairs from the sleeping porch. He told Tom, "Come on, let's dig worms."

"Can't," Tom said briefly, "I'm fixing my scrapbook." He frowned with concentration while he cut a clipping from yesterday's newspaper.

Out went Terry's lower lip. "Did old Whit get

his picture in the paper again?" he asked.

Tom nodded. "With his violin."

Tina and Merry entered in time to hear the word "violin." "Who?" they chorused and rushed to the kitchen table.

"Colin Whitney Blake," Tom said. His tone implied, "Who else?"

Tina reached the table ahead of Merry. She scanned the news story under the clipping. "His mother is entertaining guests," Tina explained. Her eyes began to shine. "Look who is in the picture—the governor's wife!"

"With *Whitney?*" Merry squealed.

Terry pushed his hands in the hip pockets of his shorts. He swaggered to Tina's side to read over her shoulder. With much satisfaction he said, "Guess old Whit will have to stay home today. Isn't that just too bad."

When Merry shook her head, her dark braids bounced. "He's coming today and bringing his water goggles with him. We are going to look at the fish under water. It'll be fun."

Terry's voice rose. "Who said so?" he argued.

"Whitney said so," Merry retorted. "What's for breakfast? I'm hungry."

Mother and Grandma were in the living room, having breakfasted with Father and Grandpa before they drove to the store. Mother called, "Is everybody up now?"

"Penny isn't," Merry answered.

"We'll let her sleep," Mother said. When she entered the kitchen, she gave each child a cheerful good-morning caress. She carried bacon and eggs to the stove. Tina browned the toast. Merry scattered plates and silver around the table. When either Mother or Tina passed by the table, they rearranged Merry's haphazard table setting. Tom pasted the clipping in his scrapbook. Then he stood on his knees on a chair to help Tina butter toast. Terry rummaged in tackle boxes for fishing equipment. Every time Merry or Tina mentioned the Blakes, which was often,

Terry talked about worms and sinkers.

While the girls washed the dishes, Tom dusted the yard chairs and replaced the big, sun-faded pillows. Terry raked the yard. He was so anxious to finish his job and go fishing, he missed litter. When Mother sent him back to do the job again, Terry saw Tina and Merry hang up dish towels and go to the trailer.

"Change your clothes!" Terry shouted. "We're going fishing!" On the way to the trash can, Terry walked with an extra swagger. *Not Whitney Blake but Terry Tucker was in control today.*

14
Alarm!

Usually Tina and Merry changed clothing as fast as Terry himself. But today Terry waited and waited. No matter how loudly he called, they did not come out of the trailer. "Nuts!" Terry muttered.

In a fury of impatience to take control before Whitney came, Terry gathered up fishing tackle and hurried to the boat. While he stored the poles in the Tub, Terry told himself this was one day Terry Tucker was going to push old Whit out of the way. He swung around and shaded his eyes to see what was going on up in the cottage yard. Still there was no sign of Tina or Merry.

Up the path Terry ran to rummage in the

garbage pail for an empty can. Off he raced to the little swampy area where the brook flowed out of the woods and into the lake. There Terry dug fat brown worms. Once in the while Tina objected to using worms for bait. Today Terry took no chance on having Tina spoil his fishing plans. When grasshoppers clattered out of the dry grass at the edge of the beach, he trapped them under his cap. With his hand full of kicking insects, and a can full of worms in mud, Terry hurried up the beach path to the cottage.

"Meet you at the dock!" Terry yelled. As he came closer to the house, Terry saw a flash of color at the parking lot. Then he heard the familiar putt-putt of Whitney Blake's motor bike. Terry clenched his fist so tightly his grasshoppers squirmed. Angrily he tramped across the yard. *"We're going fishing!"* he shouted at Whitney, Merry, Tina, and Tom.

Merry whirled and retorted pertly, "Oh, no, we're not. Tina and I are going out in the boat with Whitney and use his water goggles."

"Who wants to watch a fish swim?" Terry yelled. He planted his feet wide apart, like a sea captain, and scowled blackly.

Merry ignored Terry's scowl. She swung her short, dark braids and insisted, "I do."

"And so do I," Tina agreed.

Suddenly Terry noticed his sisters' appearance. Merry wore her red and white striped shorts with a white blouse. She even wore perky red ribbons at the ends of her braids. Tina had brushed her hair to a golden sheen. She wore her freshly ironed white shorts with a pale blue blouse. They had not dressed to go fishing with Terry. They had dressed to impress old Whit.

Terry refused to believe his eyes and ears, so determined was he to take his sisters' attention away from Whitney Blake. He snapped, "You'll get grasshopper juice on your clothes. I *told* you to change!"

"And I told you—" Merry began.

Whitney flushed with embarrassment and interrupted. "I can come back some other day. If Terry wants to fish—"

Merry tilted her chin at an independent angle. "Grandma gave Tina and me permission to use the boat. We are *not* going to fish. If *Terry* wants to fish, *he* can stand on the dock."

Whitney shifted his weight. Unhappily he said, "I don't want to cause trouble."

Though Terry saw the lonely-pup look in Whitney's eyes, he refused to ask old Whit to go fishing. Furthermore, he would not go out in that boat and watch a bunch of fish wiggle their tails. Terry glared.

Tom had been watching and listening at the edge of the group. In a peace-making tone he said, "I saw your picture in the paper, Colin Whitney Blake."

Whitney shrugged, but he grinned at Tom.

"Want to see my scrapbook?" Tom asked.

"Tom!" Tina warned.

Terry saw red creep up Tina's neck. He saw a chance to get even with at least one Tucker for spoiling his plan. After all, that scrapbook had been Tina's idea. If she had not asked Tom to find those clippings, old Whit would not have come near the Tuckers—if old Toby had not howled, if Merry had not dropped her old music, if—Terry slammed shut a door in his mind before he included himself in the list. Slyly he said, "Yeah, Whit, you'd be surprised at what's in that scrapbook."

Whitney made a puzzled noise. "Oh?"

Tina turned her head and winked her eyelashes. Merry glared at Terry, but Tom watched his idol with wide eyes, completely unaware of the tension in the air. "There's a picture of Senator Blake in the morning paper, but I haven't cut it out," he announced.

"What's Dad doing today?" Whitney asked. He stubbed a toe against the grass, kicked up a little tuft, and carefully stepped it back into the earth. His eyes were downcast.

"I couldn't read that part," Tom told Whitney. "I waited for you to tell me."

Whitney shrugged and did not answer.

The silence grew so long, Tina forgot about her damp lashes. Completely puzzled, she asked, "Don't you know where your father is, Whitney?"

Whitney's dark eyes looked like Toby's when his feelings were hurt. "I haven't seen Dad since you were at our house," he said, not meeting Tucker eyes. "I thought he would swim and fish with me this summer, but he has been in Washington, D. C." Defensively he added, "Dad's away a lot—he has to keep in touch with his public."

In Tina's imagination everything was perfect in the house where the Blakes lived, but suddenly she was not sure. She knew she would not be happy with Father away much of the time. The house felt empty when Father worked late at the store. "What do you and your mother do, Whitney?" she asked in concern.

"Usually Mother goes with Dad. When they are on a short trip, I stay home with the housekeeper. When Dad's campaigning, I live with Ruth Ann's family and go to school. If his committee works a half-year, I change schools and go with Mother and Dad." Whitney pretended to be interested in the saddlebags on his motor bike.

To Terry's surprise he felt sorry for the boy he envied. Whitney did not have to say he had spent his playtime with the Tuckers because he was lonely. Resentful though he was, Terry could see that. Before he allowed himself to like Whitney, Terry said shortly, "We'd better get going. Fish don't bite when it gets too hot."

Merry stamped a foot. "Who's going?" she demanded.

Terry swung from Merry to Tina to Tom. Not one of them responded. Wistfully Terry looked

toward the trailer where Penny still slept,
then he flung his handful of grasshoppers and
whammed his bait can against a tree.

The minute the can left Terry's hand, Tom
reminded him in his deep-as-a-well voice, "Those
worms will die."

Angrily Terry yelled, "Then pick them up and
bury them! I don't care what happens to—to a
worm!" He stormed out of the parking lot and
into the woods, thumping packed earth with the

heavy stamp of his sneakers. A short distance from the house Terry slowed his pace, but nobody hurried to catch up with him to make peace.

Briefly Terry considered cutting through the woods to the beach and taking the boat. Common sense stopped that plan. Tina and Merry had asked for permission to use the Tub. Terry had not—and there was only one boat.

The last thing Terry wanted to do was to fish alone, but what else was there to do? No children were in the neighboring cottages this week. Mr. Pitcher's grandson was college age, and Terry's old friends, Butch and Mel Smith, were in Chicago. Terry sat on the ground with his knees stuck in the air. He flipped pebbles at a ragged white daisy.

After a while, when no petals remained on the daisy, Terry cut through the woods to the shore path. The lake lay still and blue with just enough shadows around rocks to provide good fishing. Terry loved Lake Annabelle. Its peace almost cooled the heat of his mood. Then he saw the Tub pull away from the dock with three passengers —Tina, Merry, and old Whit.

In a stew of frustration Terry turned his back on the moving boat and raced down the shore path. Alone and without permission, he was not supposed to go beyond shouting distance of the cottage, but at the moment he could not have cared less. The path rose and dipped, just above the high-water mark of the lake. Anger pushed him faster and farther than he intended. Suddenly Terry found himself at the foot of the road which ran through the woods to the Smith farm.

Morning sun was beginning to beat down on the shore path. Trees shadowed the road. Terry chose the road.

When Terry came in sight of the high-posted gate where the road entered the meadow, he began to watch for Butch and Mel. Long before he reached the farmhouse he saw Mrs. Smith in the garden. She was hoeing. In the potato field

Mr. Smith's hoe rose and fell, flashing in the morning sun. Dust rose from alfalfa when Terry waded through a field.

"Are Butch and Mel home yet?" Terry called. When the words came out, they sounded thin and lonely.

"Not yet," Mrs. Smith called back.

With his fingertips in his hip pockets, Terry cut across the alfalfa field and followed a twisting rabbit trail through bramble and brush. After a while he could see the willows on the banks of the creek which wound through the Cooper farm. Finally he reached the meadow where Old Owly's herd grazed. Terry followed the barbed-wire fence to the gate at the foot of the lane.

Longingly Terry thought of the small, rock-bottomed pools under the willows. Almost invisible trout could be surprised there by flipping pebbles into the water. Well—there was nothing else to do at the moment.

Impulsively Terry opened the gate, cut across the meadow, and wandered along the creek, pelting pebbles. Once in the while he managed to skip a flat rock, but most of them plunked. Each time he threw, a cow raised her head, looked at Terry, and returned to grazing.

The lake lay below the slope of the meadow and beyond a strip of young woods. He could see Tina, Merry, and old Whit in the Tub. Terry scowled and threw another pebble, harder.

Terry did not mean to hit a cow, but he did. The cow stepped aside with a jerky movement of surprise. When she moved, another cow moved, too. Soon the whole herd was moving, slow as molasses, throwing clear morning shadows on the green meadow grass.

On an impulse, just to release his temper, Terry whooped at the heels of slow, pokey Old Owly. He waved his arms and made wigwag motions like a Boy Scout practicing code. Terry leaped and ran and doubled back on his own trail, screaming like a night hawk. The cow broke into a nervous, swaying run.

Old Owly excited the rest of the Cooper cattle. The whole herd began to run down the slope, awkwardly crowding for solid footing. Terry ran to a huge maple to watch the stampede through the meadow. His heart thumped with a beat of power.

Then Terry saw a gap in the fence at the foot of the slope and realized he had left the gate open. He should close it, he knew. Anxiously he heaved a rock in an effort to head off the herd.

Terry missed Old Owly. He picked up a heavier, sharper rock and threw again. Again, Terry missed the leader, but a great, bellowing roar seemed to come out of nowhere. With a catch in his throat, Terry recognized the bellow of the herd bull. When it crashed out of the brush along the brook, Terry knew his stone had struck the bull. Sleekly red, enormous and broad, the bull thundered after his disappearing herd. The

cows had been seen several times since the day they interrupted the hopscotch game. They had seemed harmless enough, but this was the first time Terry had seen the bull.

Shaken and nervous, Terry followed at a safe distance. He breathed shallowly and rapidly while he searched his mind for a way to turn the herd and close the gate—but he had sense enough to be afraid.

With a rush the whole herd poured through the open gate and into the Cooper lane. Maybe, Terry breathed prayerfully, maybe they would head for the barn.

Old Owly was not interested in hay or shelter at the moment. She left the lane, crashed through some brush, and thundered down the shortcut through the woods which circled the summer colony. Like a stampeding buffalo herd, the Cooper cows and bull crowded, pushed, jerked heads, and bellowed down the path.

With a sickness in his throat, Terry realized

he had let loose a force he could not control. He began to run.

At first Terry ran with no plan in mind beyond that of keeping the herd in sight. Then he remembered that Anne Green's cottage, Greer Fields, was near. When he reached her path he threw one last frantic glance at the herd and raced for help.

Terry's fingers fumbled the latch and he bumped into the gate as it swung open. He flung himself down the graveled yard path and across the porch. Terry knocked on the closed door and leaned one shoulder against the wall while he tried to pull air into his lungs. At first he heard no answer, then footsteps seemed to move toward him from some far place. After forever, the door opened and Terry gasped into Anne Green's startled face, "Is—is your h-husband home? There is a b-bull—h-headed for the *beach!*"

Healthy pinkness drained from Anne Green's

face. Eyes and mouth widened when she grasped the meaning of Terry's words. "The beach?" she repeated. "No! I just left my baby with your grandmother!"

Terry stood in complete silence for just a second while he tried to figure out where each member of his family would be at mid-morning. Sickly, he realized that probably Grandma was on the beach with the Green baby, since that was her favorite place to take any child left in her charge.

Blinded by frightened tears, Terry turned away from Anne Green and started running toward the shore. Mr. Pitcher's college-age grandson might be able to help.

Wordlessly, Anne Green kept up with Terry. They found nobody in the grocer's cottage. They knocked on the doors of other cottages in the area, but found no man to help.

"We have to do something!" Terry said through gritted teeth. So tired and frightened

his head whirled with dizziness, Terry broke away from the cottages and ran down the path which followed the brook.

Just as Terry and Anne Green reached the clearing above the sandbar, Terry saw the cattle pour out onto the beach. Old Owly had fallen back. The herd bull was leading the stampede.

Comfortably seated on the sand, Grandma, Tom, and Anne Green's baby looked as small as brightly dressed dolls. Morning sun glared down on sand and water. Not even a bush stood between the people Terry loved and the bull he had stoned while angry.

Off shore, Tina, Merry, and Whitney drifted in Grandpa's boat. Tina was leaning far over the edge with her face on the water. Suddenly Merry stood up, faced shore, and waved her arms with so much excitement she rocked the boat. Tina jerked to a sitting position. Whitney sat down beside Tina.

Tina grabbed one oar, Whitney, the other, then the oars rose into the air and slapped water. The boat jerked. Again the oars rose, and when they moved back and down, they dug water at the same time. The Tub moved.

But so did the herd. Cattle fanned across the wide beach.

"What *can* those children do?" Anne Green whispered. One arm went around Terry's shoulders, and her fingernails dug deeply into his upper left arm.

Silently Terry shook his head. There was nothing he could do to stop the advance of the angry bull. He could not even yell. Grandma would not hear his warning.

15
Proud to Be Tuckers

"Row, Whitney!" Tina gasped. Both thin arms strained on one dipping oar while her eyes photographed the unbelievable scene on the sandbar. The Cooper herd which had burst out of the woods so unexpectedly came to an abrupt stop when hooves dug shifting sand. Cows rocked horns, swayed shoulders, stepped uncertainly, and bawled.

The bull did not stop. He moved out ahead of his herd. Seeming to fix his eyes on Grandma's gaudy beach hat, he put his head down and brought thunder from his throat. He pawed up sprays of sand.

"Wh-what can we do?" Merry whimpered.

Tears rolled down her cheeks.

"Make lots of noise and draw attention to the boat," Whitney advised. "We can keep out of the bull's reach. Your grandmother can grab the baby and run."

"Wh-what about Tom?" Merry quavered. "There are a lot of cows. Tom looks so little."

"Yell!" Whitney ordered.

Obediently Merry braced her feet wide to keep from falling. She wigwagged her arms. When she was able to force sound from her mouth, she found it was easy to yell. Merry's hysteria mounted with every shriek.

"Grandma is looking back now," Merry gasped.

On shore Grandma stood up and seemed to freeze in position while she grasped the extent of danger. She snatched up Anne Green's baby who had been kicking in the sun. When Grandma moved, the bull moved. He charged the beach again, paused, pawed sand, and bellowed.

The path was blocked by the herd. Sand made running impossible. Grandma, who was terrified of water, bundled the baby under one arm and grasped Tom's hand. She ran straight toward the lake. Usually the calmest of the Tuckers, though the youngest, Tom cried in frightened surprise.

Tina and Whitney rowed with all their strength. The seaworthy old Tub plowed water. Merry screamed and waved her red hair ribbons to draw the bull's eyes away from Grandma. The bull did not stop. With the bull close behind her, Grandma reached the wet, packed sand at the edge of the beach. At the top of the sloping, wide beach Terry and Anne Green pelted rocks. With sticks they beat the hips of the cattle on the edge of the herd. A few started back up the path.

Terry darted far out on the beach, threw a rock with so much force he lost his balance and went to his knees. His aim was true. His stone hit the bull.

For a split second the bull paused, stepped sideways, swung its huge red head to eye Terry in the rear and Grandma at the edge of the water.

Tina and Whitney leaned forward till their chests touched their knees. They flattened bodies on air as they reached backward and pulled. The Tub grounded.

Tom roared. The baby cried. Grandma waded and pulled Tom. Merry reached for the baby and sank to the bottom of the boat with her arms wrapped around the screaming child. Tom clutched the rim of the Tub and heaved his sturdy body into the boat. Tina and Whitney jumped to their feet and braced themselves to allow Grandma to put her arms around their necks. She clambered into the Tub.

Just as Grandma stepped, the bull's horns raked her swinging skirt and hit the side of the boat. The grounded Tub moved from the force of the blow. Instantly Whitney plunged an oar and swung the Tub afloat. Screaming with terror, Merry snatched up a fishpole and struck the bull's sensitive nose a stinging blow.

The bull swung his huge head, bellowed, and plunged again. Merry cringed and screamed. The bull stepped into a hole and had to swim. This took the few seconds time which allowed Merry to slide onto the seat to row with Tina, Grandmother to seat herself flat in the bottom of the boat with both Tom and the baby clutched in her lap, and Whitney to stand erect facing the bull. He used the fishing pole like a lance and beat a tattoo on its nose.

Silence fell on the little group in the boat while they worked at top speed to save themselves. The bull floundered, found footing on the floor of the lake, and lunged again. He came dangerously close while Tina and Merry established a rowing rhythm. So frightened no emotion colored her voice, Merry said, "He could hook his chin over the side and tip us."

"I'll turn him," Whitney answered, in the same coldly calm voice.

As Whitney struck again and again the bull tossed his head, hesitated, then turned in a clumsy circle towards shore.

"Oh, praise God for his goodness," Grandma said prayerfully. She kissed the top of the baby's head, and pulled Tom's cheek against her own. Tom reached up a plump hand to pat Grandma's face. His eyes widened with dismay. "Grandma's glasses!" he cried. "She can't see anything without her glasses!"

Merry snuffled back tears and wiped her eyes with the back of a hand. "Where are they?" she asked anxiously.

Tom's deep-as-a-well voice returned to normal when he told Merry, "The bull will step on Grandma's glasses. She left them on the sand."

"I'll get them," Merry promised briskly.

"Oh, no, dear," Grandma objected. "They aren't worth the risk."

Merry's blue eyes flashed with decision. She declared, "The cows are going back in the woods, and the bull is swimming in circles. Land on the deep side, Whitney, where you can shove off fast. I can run across the sandbar and grab Grandma's glasses."

Whitney agreed with Merry's plan and rejoined Tina. They rowed easily, now that they rowed away from the bull instead of toward him. The Tub nosed into a sand bank. Merry scrambled onto the prow and jumped. She sprinted across the sand, snatched up the glasses and ran back again before the bull lumbered onto the beach.

Safely out from shore, the children and Grandma watched the huge red animal pace and stand and pace again, uncertain of his next action. Now Old Owly was the only cow on the beach. She rocked her horns at Terry and Anne Green, took a few short, running steps, then followed the herd. Tina saw Terry turn to Anne

Green and put his head against her side. Her arms went around him, and she knew Terry was crying. Silently Tina and Whitney rowed to Grandpa's dock.

Tina's eyes caressed the loved and familiar setting: the dock, rocking on gentle waves; the wide, sun-bright beach; the green coolness of the slope, and the cottage with eaves, gables, windows and porches arranged for happy living. Why had she dreamed of impossible perfection in a mansion? Why had she placed this quick-thinking, friendly boy in that cold place when of his own free will, Whitney had chosen the cottage? Tina heaved a tremulous sigh while she discarded all the anxieties, the uncertainties, and the budding snobbishness which had darkened the summer. When she looked back she saw the blocky redness of the huge bull silhouetted on the sandbar. "Well." She faced Whitney and put a whole conversation in one word.

Whitney nodded, understanding her relief

and sense of achievement. He grinned when he drawled, "Nobody came unglued in the emergency."

Merry swung her braids and hugged her knees. "Tuckers never do!" she declared pertly.

Quick tears sprang into Tina's eyes. Merry's words had restored something valuable Tina had lost for a time—her pride in being a Tucker. Smiling mistily, she followed Grandma down the dock, across the beach, and up the path to the cottage.

Just as the group entered the yard, Terry and Anne Green burst out of the woods. Laughing and crying at the same time, the young mother ran across the sparse grass and lifted her baby from Grandma's arms. She crooned and cuddled the baby in the midst of the excited babble of voices. "How can I thank you?" she whispered to Grandma.

Mr. Pitcher's grandson came down the lane with a handful of mail. Anne Green hailed him and asked him to walk through the woods with her, then told Grandma, "I'm sure we have time to reach home before the bull leaves the sand-bar."

Terry watched Anne Green disappear into the woods, then he turned slowly. "I'm sorry, *I'm* sorry!" he declared, not bothering to wipe off the tears which slid down his hot cheeks.

"Don't worry, dear," Grandma soothed. "We're safe." She hugged Terry's shoulders and patted his back comfortingly while she talked.

Terry raised his voice to build courage to con-fess. "You don't understand, Grandma," he insisted. "It was my fault the bull chased you. I threw rocks at the cows!"

"*You* threw rocks?" Grandmother repeated, trying to understand. "But why?"

"I—I was m-mad," Terry admitted. "I w-wanted to go fishing."

Silence fell on the group, then Grandma said soberly, "How lucky you are, Terence, that nobody was hurt. You'd have carried the weight on your conscience forever."

The Tuckers moved close together in a silent pledge of forgiveness and family love. Tensions evaporated in the high-noon sun. Tina discarded hero worship. Terry shed his jealousy. Merry stood shoulder to shoulder with her twin. Tom regarded his idol with open admiration. "Colin Whitney Blake was brave," he said, deep in his throat. "He whacked the bull, right on the nose."

"I know. I saw him," Terry told Tom. Several times Terry had almost liked Whitney. Now that Grandma and Tom, Tina and Merry stood in the backyard, unharmed excepting for the long rip in Grandma's skirt, Terry felt warm friendship for the boy he had envied.

Mother and Penny came to the edge of the porch. Mother called cheerily, "What's going on out here? Secrets?"

Tina, Terry, Merry, and Tom rushed forward to form a chattering circle around Mother and

Penny. Mother's face whitened as she listened to the story of anger, danger, and rescue. "Oh, Whitney," she said in a whispering voice, "what could my girls have done without your help?"

Shyly Penny laced her fingers in Tom's. Usually Tom did not like to be touched, but he did not pull away.

Merry's moods bounced like her braids. She had been frightened. Now she was ready to giggle. Jauntily she told Whitney, "If you want

to be friends with us, Whitney Blake, you have
to know what to do in an emergency. Things
happen!"

"Don't they!" Mother breathed. She let her
blue eyes move from one child's face to another's
to make sure each Tucker was safe.

Penny glowed with such admiration and asked
such breathless questions, she felt included in
the adventure. Then her eyes darkened as she
asked, "Where is the bull now?"

"Hey! That's right!" Terry whirled to study
the thicket beyond the yard fence. "He's still out
there some place."

"That fence isn't very thick," Penny said,
paling.

"Or high," Tom declared.

"I'll call the Cooper farm," Terry volunteered.
He galloped into the cottage, with the rest of the
family right at his heels. When he turned from
the telephone he told them, "Mrs. Cooper is
sending a man to round up the herd. She thinks

we should stay in the yard till the bull is corraled."

"*I* think so, too," Penny agreed. Her thin face flushed with so much excitement, Tina was glad Penny had not been on the beach. Fright was hard on Penny.

"I'm hungry!" Tom declared. Almost accusingly he told Mother, "I don't smell lunch."

Mother tapped the end of Tom's short nose with one finger. "Smorgasbord today," she explained cheerily.

Tina helped load the kitchen table with tuna fish, peanut butter, cheese, hard-boiled eggs, pickles, potato chips, bread and butter. Even Tom stood on his knees on a chair to make his own sandwich. He spread a thick blob of peanut butter on Grandma's home-baked bread. His back was to the windows overlooking the lake, but he was first to hear an approaching motor. "A boat is coming fast," Tom said, deep in his throat.

Whitney paused with a hard-boiled egg in one hand, a pickle in the other. "It's the Lady!" he said, beginning to glow. "That means Dad is home from Washington and he wants to *see* me." At that moment Whitney did not look older than his age.

The Blake boy led the rush from the kitchen and shouted when the Lady nosed the dock, "Watch the beach! There's a bull loose!"

Lifting a paddle from his boat, the big, red-

faced senator shouted back, "Think I can fend
him off with this?"

"Hah! *I* managed with a fish pole!" Whitney
retorted. Gay banter was tossed from father to
son and back again, revealing their gladness to
see each other.

Within a few minutes Whitney's parents were
included in the sandwich-making group in the
cottage kitchen. Tina saw that Mrs. Blake did
not even notice the fishing tackle, safey belts,
jackets, and jump ropes which hung from the
walls. Eyes, so like Whitney's, sparkled when
Mrs. Blake said, "I've been wanting to come to
this end of the lake. When I'm tired, I think of
your woods and beach and envy you the peace
and quiet."

"Quiet!" Merry gasped and clapped her hand
over her mouth to smother a giggle.

A shout of laughter greeted Mrs. Blake's
statement and Merry's response, making it
necessary to tell the story of the rescue. Tina and

Terry traded glances, knowing they had mis-
understood Whitney's mother. She had not
drawn a line down the middle of Lake Annabelle
to separate cottages from mansions. With inner
embarrassment, Tina realized she had spoiled
many happy hours by placing the Blakes on a
level with royalty. Plainly these Blakes were
home-loving people, too often separated by the
senator's official duties.

The minute the smorgasbord table was
cleared, Tom asked loudly and clearly, "Want
to see my scrapbook?"

Sudden tears stung Tina's eyes. Wishing she
could sink to the bottom of Lake Annabelle, she
began to wash cups and glasses. Everything had
been going so smoothly she had not expected
further embarrassment. What *would* the Blakes
think of that scrapbook?

"I can spell Blake, too. B-l-a-k-e," Tom
announced.

With pleased surprise Whitney asked, "How

did you learn to spell my name?"

Proudly Tom boomed in his deepest Grandfather voice, "Tina taught me. She teaches me anything I need to know."

Tina blushed. She had begun to like Whitney Blake for himself and not because he lived in a mansion with towers and had a senator for a father. Oh! Now he would think she was a boy-crazy idiot. How could she tell Whitney it was not the boy but the father's position that had impelled her to ask for those clippings? That would insult Whitney personally, and it would make her seem snobbish. "Oh, Tom!" Tina moaned, deeply embarrassed.

When Tina reached for another glass, she met Terry's eyes. He looked sorry about something. To her surprise Terry blurted, "Tom doesn't have time to hunt for his scrapbook. He's going fishing with me!" Terry grabbed Tom's arm and pulled him through the kitchen door so fast Tom tripped over the threshold.

"I've got time," Tom insisted sturdily.

"The fish poles are in the boat," Terry argued. "All we have to do is dig some worms. *Come on!*"

The screen door slammed and Terry pulled Tom across the porch, arguing noisily.

Tina ducked her head to hide her burning cheeks, but looked up when something tick-tacked the window above the sink. There stood Terry, grinning in a glad-sorry way. Terry made an O sign with a thumb and middle finger, then ducked out of sight.

"Thank you, Terry," Tina whispered to a handful of soapsuds. "Oh, thank you!" Once again she had been saved from the embarrassment of showing that scrapbook. After she swallowed her pride and talked to Tom, it would never happen again. "I'll teach Tom to spell Tucker," she vowed. "He will like that."

At the end of the long kitchen Merry and Whitney acted out the rescue scene to amuse

Penny. They pretended Toby was the angry bull, while Sugar was Anne Green's baby. When Sugar refused to lie still, Whitney sputtered, "It's harder to pretend than it was to fight the bull!"

Mrs. Blake, the senator, Grandma, and Mother applauded and laughed. Then Mrs. Blake stood and held out one hand to Mother, the other to Grandma. "Thank you for letting us share your smorgasbord, and thank you for your kindness to my son. I won't forget it. My dearest friends are the people who open their doors to my son when we are forced to neglect him. I know he's enjoyed his visit."

"I must say, he has good taste in people!" the senator boomed.

"Thank you," Mother said.

A few minutes later the Blakes sped down the middle of Lake Annabelle, flinging up roostertails of spray. The Tuckers waved and shouted from Grandpa's boat dock.

Merry stopped in the middle of a good-bye to turn on Tina and Mother. Outrage shone in her blue eyes. "Mother, you *know* Terry was RUDE the way he pulled Tom away right in the middle of a conversation!"

Mother's eyes misted. "Yes, dear," she said softly, "but it was a very kind rudeness. I am glad Terry loves Tina enough to protect her pride."

After a sober moment of reflection, Merry smiled so warmly the invisible door with no knob opened wide to welcome Terry back to twinship. She cupped her hands around her mouth and shouted at Terry and Tom who were crossing the beach with worm cans in their hands, "Wait for me! *I want to go fishing!*"

Before she left the dock, Tina saw a man drive the bull from the sandbar. Except for hoofprints punched in the sand, and Grandmother's torn skirt, no trace remained anywhere of anger or of danger.

Penny bounced on the catwalk. "What shall we do next?" she asked gaily.

Tina smiled and laid her arm across Penny's shoulders. "Who knows?" she asked.

Whitman CLASSICS

FRECKLES
Gene Stratton Porter

LITTLE WOMEN
Louisa May Alcott

LITTLE MEN
Louisa May Alcott

TOM SAWYER
Mark Twain

HUCKLEBERRY FINN
Mark Twain

BLACK BEAUTY
Anna Sewell

HEIDI
Johanna Spyri

TREASURE ISLAND
Robert Louis Stevenson

FIVE LITTLE PEPPERS AND HOW THEY GREW
Margaret Sidney

ALICE IN WONDERLAND
Lewis Carroll

REBECCA OF SUNNYBROOK FARM
Kate Douglas Wiggin

AN OLD-FASHIONED GIRL
Louisa May Alcott

TALES OF EDGAR ALLAN POE

Here are some of the best-loved stories of all time. Delightful...intriguing...never-to-be-forgotten tales that you will read again and again. Start your own home library of WHITMAN CLASSICS so that you'll always have exciting books at your finger tips.

Whitman

REG. U.S. PAT. OFF.

Whitman ADVENTURE and MYSTERY Books

Exciting, Realistic Stories...The Kind You Like Best!

THE TUCKERS

Wonderful House
Special Secret
The Adventures of Plum Tucker
Trouble on Valley View
The Cottage Holiday
Tell a Tale of Tuckers
The Turn-About Summer
Here Comes a Friend!

THE TEEN NOVELS

When Sara Smiled
The Charmed Circle
Milestone Summer
"Minnow" Vail
Then Came November
Practically Twins
When Debbie Dared
The Wishing Year

Adventure Books for GIRLS...

TRIXIE BELDEN

The Secret of the Mansion
The Mysterious Code
The Black Jacket Mystery
The Mysterious Visitor
The Red Trailer Mystery
The Gatehouse Mystery
The Mystery Off Glen Road
The Mystery in Arizona
The Happy Valley Mystery
The Marshland Mystery
The Mystery at Bob-White Cave
The Mystery of the Blinking Eye

NURSES THREE

A Career for Kelly
First Assignment
A Very Special Girl